RON PULLINS

DOLLARTORIUM

Unsolicited Press
Portland, Oregon
www.unsolicitedpress.com
info@unsolicitedpress.com
619–354–8005

DOLLARTORIUM

ISBN: 978-1-963115-66-6

This work is a piece of creative nonfiction, broadly interpreted. Elements of fiction are interwoven with the memories, experiences, narratives, and details presented within these pages. These might be characterized as autofictions or perhaps as inevitable outcomes of the inherent imperfections of memory and human perception. It is sufficient to say that, at some point, these accounts were inspired by a version of the truth.

Distributed by Asterism Books
https://asterismbooks.com/

For wholesale orders:
Asterism Books
568 1st Avenue South, Ste 120
Seattle, WA 98104
(206) 485-4829
info@asterismbooks.com

Cover Design: Kathryn Gerhardt
Cover Photo: Carlos Chavez, Tucson
Editor: Summer Stewart

To
Leslie, my dear partner

DOLLARTORIUM

Part 1

HEAVEN IS A CORN DOG

Ralph makes corn dogs. Yes, he does. From scratch. That is to say, he grows his own corn and raises his own pigs, and from those pigs he creates Ralph's famous Corny Doo Dogs—weenies impaled on little sticks, dipped in cornmeal batter, deep fat fried, hung to dry, then sold to folks who come for lunch at his Corny Doo Doggery—we recommend a squiggle of mustard along the top. They are also good plain, so have them like you want them—the always tasty Corny Doo Dog—because—as Ralph says—when you see them dipped, you know they're fresh, never frozen, and fresh is something you just don't get in stores these days. No. Not in corn dogs. Not in nothing.

Homegrown pork. Stone-ground corn. Dipped right there in front of you. That's the ticket.

Standing there on Main Street in the morning, you can look in the window of Ralph's corn dog store as the locals often do to see them dipped. Many get up early sometimes to watch Ralph work.

His daughter Stella helps, a strapping, young, good-looking woman, barely twenty, who dips the weenies in the batter, hands them to Ralph who fries them in lard. The lard is fresh and hot, crystal clear, made from the fat rendered from

Ralph's own pigs. Then Stella hangs the corn dogs up to dry. Not to cool. Oh, no. They're at their very best when eaten warm.

Ralph raises pigs on his farm out back. A crew will come by to help him slaughter his fat pigs. They cut the porkers up, grind the choicest parts which Ralph and Stella stuff into fresh casings—cleaned and washed— also made from the innards of those very pigs. He stuffs them, twists them, ties them off, then hangs the wieners in the smokehouse overnight. Yum! Yum! You'll not forget the smell of Ralph's smoked weenies. No. Then early the following morning they're dipped in cornmeal, cooked and thus become Ralph's famous Corny Doo Dogs.

He grows his corn out back as well in the cornfield behind the sty. Stella grows the corn. She plants it in the spring, fertilizing it with droppings from the pigs, cultivates it all summer, then harvests it, so once it's dried, and shucked, she grinds the corn to meal which she mixes with other stuff— exactly what is in the mix is a Corny Doo trade secret—that becomes the batter into which they dip the wieners on a stick.

Today Ralph wears his paper hat and apron, and he plays to the admiring crowd on Main who look in his window and wait for his shop to open.

You should also know Ralph loves his Plato. He is constantly reading one of many of Plato's dialogues on how to think and conduct one's life. He keeps his current read, as usual, open on the counter as he works. Truth be told, Ralph prefers to read philosophy more than work, feeling the world and his mind can always be improved with some serious contemplation.

When he cannot read or study—say, he's busy dipping

dogs—he can still think Platonic thoughts, even while sleeping, walking, talking, making corn dogs, grinding corn to meal, killing pigs. He will turn the words of his most recent read over in his mind, again and yet again, seeking some point he might have missed before, or for some new argument among the shadows and complexity of Plato's thoughts, so, even though he has no one with whom he can debate as he grinds pork into weenie meat—fortunate Socrates can dialogue with students on his front porch—Ralph joyfully debates with himself alone, catching a paragraph or two of thoughts on friendship, fidelity, truth, proof, and poetry while the grease drips from his dogs.

You'd think a man so happy, so admired, and so locally renowned—he is—would be among the richest men on earth. But Ralph is not a modern businessman. His profits are quite modest. He does not skimp on what he puts into his corn dogs. He spares no expense on pigs or corn. His dogs are quality, made daily, with no fillings, no plastic added, no sand, no sawdust, no chemicals, and never frozen (God forbid!). He keeps his prices fair, so even the poorest of the hungry in this little town can feast upon the product of his labor. Ralph revels in what he makes and in the process of his making it.

Nor does Ralph indulge in modern marketing. No bait and switch with him, no phony coupons, no 'Would you like some fries with that?' He creates nothing but the purest corn dog. He puts his heart into his work and keeps it affordable for all.

It sometimes happens a customer from out of town makes his way to Ralph's shop, and this stranger asks how one might get Ralph's dogs, say, in faraway Chicago, or Seattle, or in walks some big old Texas dude who wants his oil crew to feast on 'them there corny dogs'—perhaps he's got this annual barbeque for some good old boys, and he'd like to serve some of 'them there lip-smacking thangs …' At that Ralph says, 'Good sir, what you see is all I got. We make them every day, we sell them fresh, and piping hot, and we sell them all. If some leftovers come to be—which sometimes happens, more by design than conditions of the market—we give those freely to those who are without.'

The Mrs. Ralph—Phyllis, Ralph's wife—fumes at that. She knows there's money to be made that Ralph will never make. Modern money, too. Lots of money. Good cool cash. More than he's making now. The kind of money a modern businessman should make if he expects to please his wife and get ahead. That is to say, ahead of everybody else. That is to say, richer than everybody else.

The fact is, Phyllis is eager to get rich. Why not? She is American, she's proud to say, and she is certain that Americans like her deserve all the things Americans can get. And perhaps a little more than anybody else.

'These are perfect corn dogs, Ralph,' his customers often say. And Ralph agrees. He likes to tell a story of how years ago the gods on Mount Olympus demanded food—their nectar! ambrosia! grog!—when they were, in fact, served Corny Doo Dogs from Ralph's Corny Doo Doggery. The gods were pleased.

Well, that's a myth, but Ralph likes to tell it. It always gets a chuckle.

We see Ralph lives an honest life within his modest means, as does Stella, his lovely daughter who works happily with her daddy, carrying on the Corny Doo tradition. She also feeds the pigs and farms the corn. That is to say, she works as hard as he does.

But unhappy Phyllis is plotting change. Dangerous as any change might be, she is tired of being poor, or at least of feeling poor. The part Phyllis plays in this small enterprise is to run the register, deal with the money, take it in, count it out, give out change, pay the bills, and take what's left when day is done and put it in the bank where it can rest until she figures out how to spend it. Touching money, feeling it, counting it all day, perhaps that is what has brought her to her current state of mind where she sees things differently than Ralph and their delightful daughter.

Phyllis takes great joy in cash. Money. Paper. Profit. Promises. Debt. Deceit. This has created a great desire in her. A hunger. But not a kind of hunger which might be sated with a Corny Doo. You cannot squiggle mustard on a dollar bill and eat it. Her hunger is more abstract, and darker still, an attitude which borders on the sinister.

Such then are the seeds of conflict that have been germinating in the Doggery and will soon take root among these three. We begin to see these conflicts grow, even now, as lunch approaches.

BEGINNING THE BEGINNING

Let's imagine we're in Kansas, in some small town. Let's say a few cars are parked along Main Street, made of brick. There's not much traffic here. Occasionally a truck roars through loaded with corn or bales of hay, or a farmer comes to town to buy a part to fix his plow, or a retired couple takes their morning walk along these pleasant storefronts.

There are shops like Ralph's in every small town in America, a window facing out on Main, people looking in to see what's going on. If not a corn dog shop, then any shop that makes things, or repairs shoes, or sells handmade ice cream, coffee, sodas, popcorn, candy, or notions stores that sell hankies, scarves, and other gifts for grandma. That sort of thing.

When they walk by Ralph's, many stop to watch him prepare for his corn dog day.

We find Ralph at work this morning. He has come downstairs to get the kitchen ready, and as he does, he takes up reading Plato from where he left off yesterday. He carries his current dialogue around as he heats up pots of grease and sets out wooden sticks to skewer dogs made from the hogs he slaughtered just last week. He wears his baker's hat—as the law requires—and an apron—as his wife requires—to keep corn meal off his clothes.

Stella has come in from feeding pigs. She fills the napkin holders, and refills the mustards, moves signs to the sidewalk which invite customers to 'Come on in, The Doggery is open.'

"Daddy," she chides her father, his nose deep in Plato. "Are we cooking yet?"

She has startled Ralph. He's not near ready to begin the day, but that's her gentle way of getting his attention. She doesn't mind his reading all his books, or even when he sometimes discusses Plato's obtuse thoughts, or when he reads long quotations that make no sense to her. But when there's work to do, dogs to make, and customers at the ready, Stella takes charge and moves her father to focus more on the corn dog action. He doesn't mind. Corn dogs are the now. Plato is forever.

"Yes, dear. We're cooking," Ralph replies. He closes the dialogue, but his lips move silently as he continues some philosophical debate.

Some of Ralph's books have green covers, some blue, one is even red. This morning he reads a green one—*Plato on the Good*. Ralph continues to puzzle through this current dialogue, arguing a case, thinking first this way about all that, then that way about all this, then agreeing with the inquisitor, then finding something he disagrees with, then finding some clever way to prove who's right, who's wrong, then he takes up some forgotten and inconsequential point from Plato's latest convoluted argument, just to show how even minor details make all the difference in what is Good, and what is Not.

As Ralph debates, he lays out wieners, impales each on his

pointy sticks—'C'mon, you little doggies'—checks the grease temperature, and prepares to dip and fry. He tightens the ties on his white apron with the bravado of a matador and adjusts the chef's hat on his head just so.

His wife, Phyllis, has forbidden Ralph to read Plato when the Doggery is open. "None of that crap where people outside can see you," she says. "Customers don't come to buy your philosophical gibberish, so don't start any arguments with them. Plato makes no sense to most of us. And he makes our customers nervous. Sell corn dogs, Ralph. Go faster. Faster! And today, ask them to go for our Buy One / Get One Half-Price deal."

Before they open, Phyllis has come downstairs to ready the register, count out the money, adjust the tape, reset the counters. She likes to see the sales mount up each day. She leaves the work of making things to her husband and her daughter. Let those two serve up the dogs and clean up the mess when lunch is over. She prefers to be in charge of financial matters—she likes that fine—ringing up the orders, taking cash, making change, counting up the take, and then taking money to the bank. She keeps to her stool at the front end of the store near the register and the exit. When she's not busy, she is talking on the phone, or complaining to whoever listens, or shopping for something personal on the computer, or she is—and this is the best part of her day—catching the latest episode of *The Price is Right* or *Let's Make a Deal*, because from where she sits—there by the register—she can watch the television and play along with guessing how much things cost, which door to choose to get the prize, or what might be her final answer.

She especially loves *The Price is Right*, which she has on

now, or other shows like it.

"On the Good," Ralph says to himself. "On the Good. I say, the Good. What is the Good? And how, I ask you, does the Good emerge from the One?"

"Get to dipping doggies, Daddy," Stella says. "We need those doggies fresh, and we'll need a lot of them right away. Look outside."

"Take the money! Take the money," Phyllis says to the game show she has on television.

Stella points to the front window.

"Our customers are lining up, and they look mighty hungry this morning."

Stella has wiped the counters until they shine. She straightens up the napkin holders.

Ralph turns his book to rest face down, so he can easily find the page he has been reading. There he will resume his debate with Plato on the Good. Without much thought he starts to dip the dogs, first in the cornmeal batter, then in the grease that foams and froths. From time to time, in between the cooking and the dipping, he picks up his book and reads another paragraph, then whispers to himself, or argues with this philosopher who died two thousand years ago.

"The 'Good,' indeed," Ralph mutters with such emphasis that anyone who hears would know 'Good' is capitalized. "The Good is in the One," he continues.

He speaks towards Stella, but she barely listens.

"Or the One is in the Good. What about that, Stella?"

"That's nice, Daddy," Stella says. "We need more plastic forks. And check the mustard."

The conflicts here should be clear by now—irreconcilable desires between Ralph, Phyllis, and their Stella, while a hungry crowd gathers, time marches on towards noon, not to mention the issues of the Good, the inherent conflicts of capitalism, the odds of treasure behind this door or that, the lure of television and money and how these things connect. Ralph and Phyllis will surely collide, if not today, then tomorrow. And we can only imagine what Stella's role will be when calamity descends upon the serene world of Ralph's Corny Doo Doggery, for Stella loves her mother as much as she loves Ralph. Calamity is certain to befall them, as, of course, it is certain to fall on all good things in our small imperfect world.

Will the story end in tragedy? Is a happy resolution even possible? We'll never know until it ends, but at least for now we've seen the layout of the beginning.

THE MASTER ARRIVES

Phyllis watches *The Price is Right*, sitting at the register.

People getting rich for no logical reason is her idea of happiness. People on *Let's Make a Deal* pick a door. Or a box. Or a curtain. They come to the studio dressed in funny clown outfits, floppy shoes, red balls on their noses. That's funny, isn't it? Look at that man and woman couple. They are wearing signs. Hers reads *Us! Us! Us!* His reads, *If not Us, Me! Me! Me!* That's funny, too. The gameshow host, a microphone near his lips, can barely stop his laughing.

"You! You! You!" the host calls out. "Ha, ha, ha. Pick a number, one, two or three."

"Pick a number! Pick a number!" Phyllis sits on the edge of her stool, braced against the cash register.

"Any number?" Ralph asks. One can hardly avoid overhearing Phyllis in their small shop.

"Not you. Them!" she says. "They're about to make some money, if they are lucky."

Phyllis talks to Ralph without looking away from the television.

"But what does it mean?" Ralph asks.

"Oh, Ralph," she says. "Must everything mean

something?"

She loves game shows of chance and money. She loves to see contestants pick a random number, choose a door that suits their fancy, turn a wheel, or guess a letter of the alphabet to complete a phrase. Oh! *Wheel of Fortune*, great God of Luck! Then, for whatever random reason, they win some random thing. Everyone wins something. Anything. Some win small, some win big, but they all win something, and without any work, effort, or knowledge. No skill is required there, only luck. No imagination is required to turn mediocrity into cash, or into things, or pleasure, on her favorite game shows.

"Take the money! Take the money!" Phyllis blurts out, as the pair of clowns are given a choice between some certain cash or an unknown prize. To a devotee of luck in all its forms, as Phyllis is, such shows make bourgeoise life almost bearable.

"Open the door, Stella," she says without taking her eyes off the show. "It's time to open the Doggery."

Phyllis keeps to her place beside her register, her niche during the noon rush, her aerie, the best place from which to watch television, and the store's nexus for money, that crossroads where corn dogs become cash. Phyllis might bag a few corn dogs—if they get busy, although she hesitates to waste pennies on free paper bags, napkins, or mustard. But she enjoys her task of making the register ring, changing big bills into smaller ones, and dollars into cents, and watching a pile of cash grow in her register as the corn dogs find their way into the gullets of their customers. It is a great joy to realize at day's end they have more money than they had at the beginning.

Ralph puts down his book.

"We got a few more minutes, dear," he says.

Ralph doesn't hear the television or notice his wife's smile, nor would he react much even if he saw the television, engrossed as he usually is in Plato. Phyllis listens to the gleeful emcee on TV, and to all the happy, potential winners who hop up and down with enthusiasm, waving their winnings—cash and coupons, or keys to a new car, or holding a brand new air fry cooker—as if they had actually earned something, waving stuff—like a weekend in Las Vegas—which they win if they opt for the right curtain instead of taking the cash.

Phyllis desperately wants her life to get better as she sees life getting better for these game show winners. Such is the promise of television, on which she models her dreams. Phyllis feels wealth is all she needs to have a better life, however it is acquired. And as much as she rates her life now in the shitcan, the better she knows it will be when and if she gets rich. She will get rich! Her mind is bent on it.

She is no maker of corn dogs. That's for sure. Her hands are too delicate. Her manicure is too expensive. She doesn't know how to poke a stick up the end of a dog, wiggling that pointy thing into the bottom of the meat and then running it through, and she doesn't want to know how to do it. Her skin hurts when it's splattered with hot grease, so she avoids those grease pots. And someone does have to run the register. Why not her? Someone has to handle the cash. Otherwise, Ralph would give away those Corny Doo Dogs and all the profits. Anyway, to Phyllis's way of thinking, it's not a woman's place to grind pork, cultivate corn, or feed pigs. At least not *her* place. It's enough to have married a man who does that sort of thing. She is happy to commit her beloved daughter to such work as well. Stella likes it. Let those who like it do the dirty work.

Phyllis avoids talking to friends about her husband's work, or the work he does, or what she thinks about it. Better it would have been for her if Ralph had become a lawyer or a financier. As things are, when she must say something to her friends about Ralph, she says, "Well, my Ralph is in the food industry," hoping strangers might imagine Ralph is perhaps a financial officer for Nabisco, or that he writes advertising copy for Little Debbie cupcakes.

Phyllis doesn't like selling corn dog things. She doesn't like selling anything. Sales is so commonplace and the exchange of cash so ordinary. Especially cash for corn dogs. I mean, pig meat fried in pig grease. But she does love having cash. She loves cash when it comes to her at the end of that long chain of effort others do. When her friends ask her what she does, she says she is in charge of financial things. "You know," she says, "I deal with banks." Meaning, in fact, she puts the day's take in the night deposit box.

She imagines herself to be a capitalist. She sees her role in life as being the taker of money from the consuming class for goods made by the producing class, all for the good of the financial class. That's so very modern, being a broker between the classes, between inputs and outputs, while never having to get dirty. She is happy to oversee the process of consumers getting Product in exchange for Cash. She is happy to discuss Value and Worth. She loves Marketing. Each day she keeps track of Sales by the hour, and, when things are slow, she draws data points on charts, lines that point from what things have been to what things might yet be. She happily and mechanically thanks customers for their purchases because she believes that greeting consumers will increase sales, which will improve her charts, which in turn will move her closer to her dreams. What little she can save, she invests in stocks, even investing in giant food chains which daily become more powerful and profitable and someday will try to buy up Ralph's Doggery, in which case she will benefit both by all that cash and then by their rising stocks. With all that wealth, there will no need to work—if you call sitting at the register watching television work. Her duty is to get Ralph on a clear path to fortune before some competitor destroys the Doggery.

From time to time, she involves herself in the idea of the Product, how to make it, how to speed up how it is made, how to cut the cost of making it, however much her ideas annoy Ralph and Stella. "Maybe if we make the dogs a little smaller," she's suggested. "Add a little fat which is cheaper than the meat. Who will know the difference?" She is overflowing with ideas for others to implement while effortlessly increasing her pile of cash.

Ralph rarely listens to her. He's got his Plato. Stella is too busy doing what she loves to pay much attention to either parent.

So, Phyllis has passed the years watching television and dreaming of winning, wishing her life was more like that of a game show contestant—like that one there now dressed as a giant bee—how funny is that? "I knew you'd get a buzz." Ha, ha, ha.

Cash has a beauty you can't find in corn dogs. Cash tracks well on charts. Cash measures the Good. Cash is the Good; who doesn't believe that? Cash improves one's credit score and thus opens the door for even more cash, more Good. Cash never gets old. Cash never grows moldy. Cash doesn't need cooking, killing, feeding, or washing down. Cash does not need planting, weeding, or harvesting. Cash can buy anything worth buying. Everything she wants. One can never have too much cash. It's easy to store. And, unlike corn dogs, too much cash does not make your stomach ache.

Unfortunately, Phyllis likes to spend cash, too. She likes to buy things she likes, things she needs, things she doesn't need. She loves the process of buying things for cash and selling things for cash. She loves the way cash feels before she spends it, the way it smells, how it tastes—yes, from time to time, she'll taste a coin. Haven't we all? She even likes the word, 'cash,' how it forms in the throat like a gasp and hisses through the teeth. She likes saying it. She likes telling people how much she wants it. She likes thinking of having a lot of it, bags full of cash, enough to swim in. So much that even when she has everything she'll ever need, she'll have cash left over—lots of cash—to show people she could buy more, and maybe she will, after all. Cash is good, and the more the better, lots is best of all. It fills her up, at least for some short while. Cash populates her dreams.

But it's a long way from her dreams to where Phyllis sits today watching contestants less worthy than her getting rich. Not that she will change, but she thinks Ralph should be more ambitious. He should work harder, longer, more effectively, and all that for more profit. She would like a new house, and a guest house out back would be nice. A pool, too. And a hot tub like the neighbors have. And a garden with flowers. And a gardener to take care of it.

She certainly needs—and deserves—a new car. A servant to cook dinner. A boy to care for the pool. Matching cherubs on the bathroom wall to go along with the mirrors she bought at Macy's. Once she has reached this status, of course, she will need money for society events—you know, events to 'help the poor' and to 'elevate the middle class' and to 'elect more Republicans' so she won't have to pay those damned taxes. She would also like to take a cruise on a liner, with a cabin, which would have a view her neighbors can't afford. And, oh, yes, finally, a poodle.

She has none of this now. Just a two-bedroom apartment above Ralph's modest Corny Doo Doggery which she shares with Ralph and their daughter Stella. No, it doesn't even have a fireplace.

A fireplace would be nice, she thinks, as she watches *The Price is Right*. They are giving away a fireplace if your guess is the closest as to what the thing costs.

Stella is on the back line preparing food. She washes the counters off, she turns the pots on—pots of grease and corn dog batter, testing, tasting, taking temperatures, wiping the stainless steel counters until they shine—and she checks to make sure Ralph isn't lost again in reading Plato. Stella wears jeans and a long shirt as she works. She also dons an apron and a paper hat. Her sleeves are rolled up. Grease splatters on her forearms, all part of the job.

Stella looks lovely this morning, as always, no makeup and a smile.

Stella loves making corn dogs. She loves hearing customers say nice things about what they make. She even looks forward to cleaning up after the store closes. The greater the mess, the better their day has been providing pleasure for their neighbors. She looks forward to tomorrow and to doing it all again.

Soon she will open the store, and before that—well, even now if we look outside the big plate glass window—out on the sidewalk, out along Main Street, folks are lining up, looking over the menu posted in the window, deciding on what they will order, how they will fix their own corn dogs for themselves, or for friends back at the office who have sent them out to pick up lunch.

"Keep 'em cooking, Daddy," Stella says.

Ralph impales the dogs on sticks, dips them in the batter, then dips them in the grease. His Plato, the green book, is open before him. The window is near the grease pots so Ralph can look up and see the crowd staring at him. He waves.

"You see them dipped, you know they're fresh!" he says, even though they cannot hear him through the glass. They know the slogan; it's painted on the window. Ralph is proud of that line. He invented it himself. He is sure it is one cause of their success. Outside the crowd grows hungry.

"Look, Ralph," Phyllis says. She points to the television. "It's door three. Door three! I knew it! I could have had a new car, Ralph. A red luxury sedan. Oh, Ralph, I'd like a new car. We should raise our prices."

She will continue this theme throughout the day.

"Or we could extend our hours. Just a few more customers," Phyllis says. "There's got to be a few who'd like a corn dog dinner. 'A corn dog meal for Two.' We could run a special. Or for Three! 'Take a corn dog home for Baby.' 'A corn dog for the dog!' I love it. Or sell your corn dogs to restaurants, Ralph," she continues. "I wish you were more aggressive, Ralph. You could freeze your corn dogs, then sell them to grocery stores."

With a heavy finger she rings in the register, and the drawer slides open, and then she whacks a roll of quarters on the edge to fill the slots with coins.

"Or sell them through Amazon. I don't know why we don't sell our corn dogs on Amazon. Or why we don't add desserts to our menu, Ralph. People like desserts. A pudding, perhaps. Or a corn dog souffle. Or those little pies fried in grease. I bet we could sell a lot of pies like that. Use that same pig grease, of course. No need for new grease. A Corny Doo Doggie Apple Pie. Or make and market our own mustard. Maybe you could package our pig grease. And …"

Her voice trails off as the commercial ends and the current game show resumes.

"Come on down!"

Phyllis hugs the cash register as if it were a lifesaver and she were awash in an ocean of corn dogs. But she accidentally flips the channels and abruptly lands on an infomercial. There the television is stuck. She cannot change the channel. Her clicker doesn't work. It has stopped on a show with a funny man in a funny suit of red and blue stripes, a hat with silver sparkling stars, paper money stuck all over him like feathers on a bird. His image fills the screen, and he is dancing and singing about how easy it is, how necessary it is, how natural it is, to be greedy, to be rich, so in the end—as he sings, and taps his cane, spins and taps across the stage, this way and that, shedding dollar bills like leaves in September falling from trees—so much money stuck to him he needs to never do work, never have obligations, never suffer from any unfilled needs—let thine piggybank runneth over—all the money he wants to buy all he wants, so much he has of what others can't have because he has it all. Ha, ha, ha! How much fun! Imagine the joy. The man on the television sings, he smiles, he dances and taps his way back across the screen, then the other way, and money flutters from his clothing to the ground, like leaves from a money tree.

Phyllis stops trying to change the channel and is fixed on watching this little green man.

Ralph smiles and reads Plato, not noticing her or him at all, nor does he pay attention to the eager crowd waiting at the door. He nods.

"The Good is the Form," he says under his breath, because Stella is working and she won't listen, and Phyllis, if she hears, will ignore him. "And the Form is the One."

Ralph blinks.

"Now there is a puzzler," he says, as he tries to make sense of such an abstraction.

Phyllis only hears the voice on the television, hears the promise of money and the things one can get with it. Ralph glances at a passage in his book, then looks up, smiles at the faces outside the window, customers watching him dipping and frying. He waves. His customers, after all, are mostly his friends. He is part of this community. Phyllis stares at the television, at the man in spangles, and he waves again, as if he were a customer.

"What?" she says. Then she waves back at him. The man on TV looks like a very nice man, someone who knows exactly what he wants and is going to get it.

"Out there! Out there! Who wants wealth?" the man blares from the television set. "Who's out there who wants vast riches?"

"I do! I do!" Phyllis says towards the screen.

She points for Ralph to look at the set, to see the man dressed—red, white, and blue, covered in green dollars, like feathers. His hat is red, white, and blue, too. He struts around the stage, money on him so thick he sheds it as he dances, and money flutters to the ground.

"Ralph! Look! There's someone who knows something about money. Oh! He's got so much of it. Isn't he cute? Isn't he clever?"

Ralph smiles politely, a sure sign he has not been listening, not paying attention to Phyllis at all. He rarely ever pays attention to her, especially during work, nor when he has Plato to ponder, and he never ever listens to television. Ever. Television with all those commercials is maddening.

"You! And you! You all want riches!" the television man says. "Come join me all, you silly bitches."

"Riches. That would be nice," Phyllis says. She leans into the cash register, embraces it, as she stares adoringly at the television, her body language showing how much she wants to reach out and touch him, caress him, pull him out of the set and into her arms.

"You!" the man on television says again this time pointing directly at Phyllis. His voice is soft now, inviting, almost sensual.

Phyllis touches her breast.

"You mean me?" she asks.

A smile slowly comes to her lips as she realizes he does indeed mean her. He nods. He smiles, too.

"Yes, you! And you! And you! And you!" he repeats, pointing every which way, but first and last at her, especially at her so rapt in the moment. She has been chosen.

"Well, yes," she says. "I want that. I mean, riches … I mean, wealth … I mean, status. Power. Glory. Whatever you are giving out. Whatever you are promising. I love you," she says, even if she doesn't quite know what she's saying.

She stands up, and with a proper, attentive posture looks at the television with full attention.

Outside, through the window, on the street, people who have been watching Ralph turn to see the television. They have an eager, hungry look. Stella is about to unlock the door, but the man in the television, his look, his invitation, has made time stop.

Outside the customers stop moving. Inside the corn dogs stop cooking. Stella moves, but she is totally involved in the moment preparing corn dogs. Ralph is reading his Plato.

"Good there, then, my little honey," he says. He points to Phyllis. "We have some time. Let's make some money!"

With that he leaps out of the television, hops onto the counter, then off the counter onto a stool, then off the stool and onto the floor, all in one continuous and graceful set of leaps and bounds, his demeanor a study in happy anticipation.

"You're with me, then, dear sweetheart?" he asks. He hugs her without asking.

INTRODUCING THE MONEY MASTER

Thus, suddenly a creature from the television set enters our world, and everything stops cold. Ralph, Stella and Phyllis are still there. The town beyond the Doggery is still there. Even the customers are still there—some of whom are inside lined up for corn dogs, others lined up outside waiting to come in— all with smiles on their faces, eager, but motionless.

Well, Ralph hasn't been stopped as he continues to read Plato and make corn dogs. And Stella continues to move about. She unlocks the door, preparing for the rush of customers, bringing out dogs to dip, and cornmeal batter to dip them in, and bags, and cokes, and cups. And Phyllis stands in awe of the creature from the television who has hopped down to her counter and sashays back and forth, to the register—but don't get too close to her register or she'll think you're a thief—then to the far end of the counter, then sashays back again.

Phyllis, too, pulls back at first, sits up on her stool, in shock, but she slowly grows more comfortable in the presence of this odd little character who has leapt from the television. In fact, she finds herself eager to reach out and touch him in some intimate way. She admires the dollars he wears and sheds like feathers, and she fluffs his coat of money which he coyly allows as he sashays by.

We can see she admires him. Someone from TV. Someone important. Someone who wears money on his coat, who cares little if some money falls off to the floor. Someone who doesn't even bother to pick up those stray dollars. Someone who pays attention to her. Someone who wants to snuggle up to her. He has his own TV program! He must be important.

"What do you want?" Phyllis asks.

"Be with me," he says.

After some hesitation she answers. "I am, I am. I'm right here. With you."

"Well, I'm here, too," he says, "And you're here. So, we're here together. And we've gotten to know each other. So maybe by now you'd like to make some money."

"Me," she says. "Well, yes," she says. She pauses. Swallows. "Yes," she says. "I want to make some money. I mean, I want Ralph to make some money. Then I would have some money. If he were rich, then I'd be rich. But he and I, we see things differently. But, money, yes, he should see things my way, shouldn't he and make the money that I need?"

She stumbles on. She has very few friends with whom she can share her feelings, so now, having found a friend who feels what she feels, her feelings pour out.

"So, if we had money," she says, "we'd have money. And I want money. So, there that is. I hope that's clear."

She ceases babbling. Then the Money Master—for such is what he calls himself, although she does not know that yet— draws closer to her. Too close perhaps. So close she cannot speak, his nose almost touching her nose.

"I see you need to make money, then," he says. "It just so

happens I have a school where I teach students how to get rich. Not all who seek admission get in. Women are welcome. It's a very special school. But, if one gets in, one learns the trade, the tricks, the ways of making deals, of making money, of getting rich, of staying rich, of getting ever richer still, and how to let everyone know it. Yes. Let me introduce myself. You see before you, Money Master."

He bows.

"Really?" she says. "School?" she says. "I've always thought school was a waste of time. Books. I mean, look at Ralph and all his books, his silly philosophy, where's that got him?" She catches her second wind. "Why, I've always said, if he'd get his nose out of all those books, if he had all the money he's paid for all those books, if he'd been working instead of reading, making pies, for instance—that's just one of my suggestions—add little pies to the menu—then I could afford that little white poodle I've dreamed about. And a house for the poodle. And a groom to do the grooming. A pool. And … But, no …"

The Money Master listens, smiles. He's heard all this before. So many stories from the poor who yearn to be rich.

"But a school for learning business and making money," she says. "If there is such a thing, I've never heard of it. I haven't been to school since I was a wee thing. Well, I'm not that old," she says, catching herself.

She brushes hair behind one ear flirtatiously, but then gives the little man a look to say she will fend him off if he dares make a pass, but … would she? She hugs the cash register, keeping it between her and her newfound friend— her new best friend forever.

The Money Master leans over the counter, his nose again less than an inch from her own.

"I'm not that young, of course," she says. "But then I'm not that old, either. But you said school … Well …"

She flushes. She looks over his shoulder and up at the television.

"Hey, how'd you get out of that television thing? How'd you get from there to here? And are you real? I thought …"

"No more thinking," the Money Master says. "Too much thinking is an impediment to action, and making money requires action. Where has all your thinking gotten you thus far?"

His voice comes out so long and low, slides up his throat and words fly out so smooth, so soft. And that tongue of his, so thin and red. She loosens her grip on the cash register, lets herself relax, then looks at him again, into his dark eyes, green eyes, as green as dollar bills, seeing something there inviting, enticing, and full of promise, as if she has known him for a long time. Maybe in her dreams. Oh, if only.

Then, as if she is waking up, she says, "So, is this a dream?"

"A dream?" he asks, rubbing some of the dollar bills that hang like feathers from his jacket. "It is *money*! Ha!" He laughs. "It is the stuff of dreams, but just as real as you or I."

He has a way of saying 'money' like it is the sweetest, most dreamy thing in all the world. And Phyllis loves it. She loves the sound of it, the way he says it, almost as much as she loves money itself. She touches his coat, the dollars, the feathers. Soft. A few dollar bills come loose. Does he see? Will he not notice? Can she have them? She doesn't ask. She slides them into her pocket.

Meanwhile, Ralph and Stella prepare for lunch. Ralph dips corn dogs, thinking Platonic thoughts, reading Plato when he can, arguing with himself, then getting back to dipping. Ralph is so engrossed in Plato he doesn't notice anything unusual. Stella hurries about, too busy working at getting things ready for the day to notice her mother being seduced and their customers locked in time.

If seduction is the right word for one so eager to be seduced.

The Money Master eyes Phyllis head to toe, as if she were not dressed at all, but feathered in dollars like himself.

"So, you are real," Phyllis says. "This is almost too good to be true."

"Real?" he says, flashing around the solid gold-headed cane he carries. "Who can doubt it? As real as the head of this cane is gold and worth as much," he says.

Phyllis says nothing. She likes the touch of gold.

"It feels like what gold should feel like," she says. "And I guess it's real if you say it's real. And worth a lot, because folks say that's true. I've never felt real gold before. I've touched the gold-plated stuff at Walmart, you know. But that's not really solid gold. And I've never really seen it up close, like this. I knew someone who had a gold filling once. If that was gold. But I didn't touch it. I wanted to. But, if you are who you are, if you are who you say you are, and you know what you say you know, well, then I like you, and I like gold, and let's be friends."

"Be my love," the Money Master says, his lips so close to her left ear he seems inside her head.

Then the Money Master backs away, and Phyllis relaxes, having been forced up against the counter, her back against the register. She sighs.

"And this place where you learn to get rich, that's real?" she asks.

"Of course," the Money Master says. "As real as any promise, as solid as any dream. And I promise you, we can make you rich. If you believe. Yes, that's the thing. I see you have the hunger. For wealth. For power. And for privilege. If you believe in me, I can make you rich. I can reveal the simple secrets to obtaining the wealth the well deserving so well deserve."

"I hope it's not too much work for me," she says.

Phyllis is adamant. She doesn't want to work. It is much better to be born into wealth. The plan right now is to get Ralph in gear.

"Work is so old fashioned," the Money Master says. "And work doesn't work so well anyway. Many who work are still poor—two, three jobs at a time, so go figure where work gets you."

He stands against the counter and admires his fingernails.

"People say only the rich can get rich anymore," she says.

She edges closer to him, and touches his shoe, for he has hopped up on the counter again. She is coy, almost flirtatious. Her face is near his feet as she looks up. But the Money Master looks at his fingernails, pretending he's somewhere far away, contemplating something no doubt important.

"So you want to get rich?" he asks, not looking at her at all.

"Oh, my yes," she says. "I'd like that a lot. I'd like to be rich. And if you know the tricks, if you have the wheel, I can spin it. Or if you ask me Door 1, 2, or 3 …"

He hops to the ground and puts his arm around her shoulder, giving her a small hug. Stella is going in and out of the Doggery getting supplies. Ralph reads his book and thinks, even as he pulls a string of golden brown corn dogs from the grease and hangs them to drip dry. The customers remain frozen in the moment.

"So, if the Good is One, then the Primal Condition is Good, and all else is Not," Ralph whispers. Then he shakes his head. "No. That can't be true. That's too easy." He wipes his hand on his apron, and then it's back to work, dipping and cooking.

"Take him," Phyllis says, pointing to Ralph. "Train Ralph. Teach him. I'm too delicate. Too busy to go to school. I don't have the background. I'm an artist. I have an appointment …"

Nearly in tears, Phyllis holds the Master's lapels, looks straight into his chest, straight at his heart—she assumes he has a heart—and strokes the dollar bills with which he is festooned.

"Make Ralph rich," she says to the little man. "Heaven knows I've pestered him for years. He needs to work harder. I say, 'Quit reading all those books.' All he does is read. Books! Books! Books! 'Read all you want,' I say. 'But make some money, too.' I say, 'This is America. The economy's booming. Get us some of that boom!,' I tell him. 'Our fair share. And a little bit more,' I say. 'That's all I want.' All Ralph does is make corn dogs and read books. He says, 'It's a living.' But I say, 'What's a living if you're poor?'"

Hands behind his back, the Money Master struts back and forth along the counter, above Ralph, then leaps to the floor and walks around him, seemingly invisible, then looking over Ralph's shoulder, then looking down at his book, then studying Ralph, sizing him up.

"Helping the few acquire great wealth is my profession," the Master says. "It's what I do. Finding the eager ones willing to do what must be done … Although …" He pauses, looks at Ralph from head to toe. "Usually, I have more material to work with. Still …"

The Money Master grabs a fresh corn dog. He smells it, squirts on mustard, and takes a bite.

"Ah!" he says. "Very tasty."

The Money Master chews while he paces. He waves the corn dog like a wand.

"I generally make more money for those who already have a lot. That's easier to do. And obviously, such people are better material to work with."

He likes this corn dog. He inspects what's left of it.

"Mighty nice corn dogs," he says. "A man who makes a corn dog as good as this ought to be rolling in dough."

"Exactly!" Phyllis says. "But you can't put a corn dog in the bank. Teach him something, please. If not how to be rich, at least how to make people think we are. We need help, Mister … Who are you again?"

"The Money Master, ma'am. Master, for short. From television. Late-night TV. Endlessly on the free channels, lost among the ads for kitchen aids, or how to cook your bacon, and the many, many mesothelioma ads. I'm especially there on early mornings when minds drift from what is into what could be. Those desperate hours.”

“You’re *the* Money Master?”

“At your service,” he says. He bows.

Phyllis bows back and offers him another dog. She’s heard of him. She’s even seen him many times and watched his infomercials. Indeed, she’s had her desperate hours of thinking this might be the answer. “Take another corn dog. And another. And another. Take all you want.”

She helps him help himself, as he pockets half a dozen. Ralph doesn’t notice. Socrates is on his mind for he has just said something witty somewhere deep in *On the Good*.

“Teach Ralph,” she says. “I’ll pay. Whatever it takes. Free corn dogs forever.” She draws nearer to him, but he backs away and mustards his second corn dog.

“Well, lady, first off,” the Money Master says, swinging his corn dog in the air to emphasize his point, “it all comes down to the deal. How to make a deal. How to deal when you deal. How to cash in on the deal once you’ve made it. How to know the cards you’re dealt, how to deal them so you win, how to fix it so you can’t lose, how to change the rules of whatever game you play. Any game. Any time. Anywhere. With anybody.”

“Exactly what he needs to know,” she says. “We’re Americans, after all. And getting rich is plenty legal. We’ve got savings. We’ve got credit. We vote Republican. We should be rich.”

Ralph sits with his elbow on the counter, his hand holding his book, while he dips dogs in corn meal with his other hand, then drops them into the grease. His lips move as he reads. He doesn’t hear Stella, or the Master who parades around the shop, avoiding Phyllis.

"I imagine Ralph will be a hard case," the Money Master says. He carries the last of his second corn dog in his cheek and wags the empty corn dog stick about. "It might cost a bit more than the normal."

"My daughter, then," Phyllis suggests. "Take her. Train her."

Stella is behind the counter now putting on her apron and cap.

"A lovely lass. Old Plato there, though," the Master says, nodding towards Ralph, "might be easier to bring around."

"I've driven us into debt, thinking that shame will make him work harder. I've run up our credit cards. I tell him the neighbors make much more than we do. I point out all the nice things they have. Our neighbors two houses down the street have a hot tub. Why, even my bathtub lacks the jets that we need to relax in these trying times. Our shop needs paint. We painted it last year, but I don't like the color. And I'd like to take a vacation someplace nice … You've seen the ads. A beach on some poor island makes you feel much richer than you are because you are not so poor as those who serve you there. But regardless of what I do, night after night Ralph comes up to bed smelling of cornmeal, grease, and pigs, and reading books. He's too happy with how things are. I deserve more. I want what greed can get us."

Phyllis looks desperate.

"We should all get all we can, we should all get all we want, and we should all want all there is, and more," she says. "Look at TV. All about the rich and powerful. Who wants to watch the poor and desperate when one can watch the rich and beautiful.”

The Money Master strokes his chin with his hand, looks up and thinks.

“It sounds like Ralph needs a money machine,” the Money Master says.

“That’s it!” Phyllis says. Suddenly now she’s alert. “Whatever that is, that’s what we need.”

“And to be trained on how to use it, of course. Maybe I just happen to have one he can buy.”

“Yes! Yes!” she says. “Train him on our own money machine.”

“That comes at some small fee for my Dollartorium where we offer classes in financial schemes, how to maximize the monetary output of our machines, and how to plug them into the great machine of progress. Also, how to threaten, sue, badger, cheat, and play golf. Learn the skills well, and one will never work another day in one’s life!”

“Take Ralph,” Phyllis says. She hugs him. “Take him to the Dollartorium. Sell him a machine. Teach him how to run it. Get him to making money. How soon can he begin?”

“Not all who go can succeed,” he warns her. “And there are dangers in running such a machine.”

She doesn’t want to hear that.

“He wants to start right away,” she says. “I’ll see to that. You bet.”

SONG AND DANCE

The Money Master is not without a philosophy or principles. He operates on how he feels and what works for him. That is enough. To think beyond thought only muddies the water.

"Richer is better," the Master says.

Phyllis is enthralled.

"Richer is good," she says.

"Always borrow as much as you can. It is better to spend other people's money than your own."

"Borrow more," she says.

"Debt is good. The deeper, the better," the Master continues. "Fine, if you can't pay it back. In fact, better to avoid paying it back at all. If you borrow enough, they'll lend you more. If you must pay back, pay back just a little. They'll be grateful. Borrow so much they can't let you fail. There is always someone with money willing to lend it. And there's always the government, too. And thus, my dear, the rich get richer."

"Ralph always pays cash," Phyllis says.

"Cash?!"

The Money Master shakes his head. Ralph is cooking corn dogs, blissfully unaware of a fate being planned for him.

"The rich never pay cash," the Money Master says. "Best if you never pay at all, no matter what you've borrowed. Just borrow more to pay them back and ask for more the second time. Let them sue you."

Phyllis sighs. Being rich is so not Ralph. But finally she has found someone who understands.

"I say to Ralph, 'Who cares about corn dogs?'" she says. "I say, 'Cut wages.' Or, 'Raise prices.' Or, 'Let's become Le Corny Deux Doggie and give the place some class.' Or 'Mass produce your corn dogs in China.' It's not like I haven't tried to get him on track to getting rich."

The Money Master clasps his hands behind his back and paces. The customers stand motionless now. Time remains at a standstill. The Master helps himself to another corn dog with mustard.

"Every morning, he ties on his apron, puts on his hat, comes down to work, and makes corn dogs," Phyllis says. "And reads Plato. That's it."

She turns to her register to get it prepared for the day. Pitiful as it may be, they must sell corn dogs. She has so many things she wants to buy.

"Greed doesn't come natural to everyone," the Master says.

"I was born to be rich," Phyllis says, breaking open a fresh roll of pennies. "If I don't get rich quick, I'll be stuck in the damned middle class."

"The way things are going, there soon won't be much in the middle," the Master says.

A roll of nickels. Crack. She pours more coins into the drawer. "I mean, I'm an American. I deserve more."

Suddenly the Master slaps his hand down on the counter.

"I'll do it," he says. "I'll make you a princess! I'll take on the project! I'll teach Ralph about greed! The tricks of the game. Someday he'll be, if not the richest there is, then still pretty damned rich. We'll build it on corn dogs. What's a more basic food than corn dogs? I love it."

"Then will I live in a castle?"

"You'll live in a castle and wear diamonds, my dear." He leans up behind her, puts his mouth to her ear and whispers, "Diamonds and jewels, horsemen and servants."

She closes her eyes and feels his warm breath. She caresses the register and rings up a sale.

"A million corn dogs," he says. "Five million or more. A billion, I say. And one billion more. Someday a trillion? Corn dogs for all, and money for you."

"I'll travel the world," she says. "Luxury liners. Sleek foreign cars." She feels him pressed up against her.

"You'll be someone, not the no one you currently are. Things'll never again be like they are now."

"Yes," she says. "I'll be someone. Not no one. I'll be somewhere. Not here."

"You'll be one of the rich who get richer and richer," he says. "Not one of the rest who never will."

"I'll get unstuck from here, from this middle class, where I've been stuck forever. If I must ever get stuck somewhere else again, let me get stuck somewhere on top."

He kisses her neck.

"You'll be where the haves will be having, and you'll be having what the have nots have not."

"Yes," she says. "I'll be in with the withs, while the rest are without."

They hold hands and dance, round and round, to a song only they can hear.

"There are masters, there are slaves."

"There's the few, then the rest."

"Owners and owned."

"Then the poor, and the best."

THE OPENING

The customers are lined up at the counter and waiting to be served. Ralph puts his book away, wraps and bags the dogs, dips and cooks more.

"You see them dipped ..." he says and smiles.

The customers pay no attention to the strange man standing on the counter near the television. They are used to the unusual here.

"Two dogs," the first customer says.

Phyllis—breathless—rings up the bill.

"I'm getting my Ralph into the Dollartorium," she says. "Have you heard? Ralph will be getting us a money machine. They're going to teach him how to run it. And I'll make sure he runs it. You can bet on that. Then won't I have money? Yes, I will. As much as I want. And a little bit more. Won't I be someone? You wait and see. That's $4.85."

In silence they pay, and Phyllis makes change.

"$7.20," she says to the next customer, "out of a ten."

She barely pauses.

"Soon I'll be getting a new BMW. A red convertible, it'll be. Ralph's going to be learning about business and wealth."

The line moves along. Everyone's eager for lunch.

"Money," Phyllis says, to the next customer in line.

"Corn dog and corn dog," the customer says, as he gets out his billfold.

"Money, and money, and more money still."

"And a squiggle of mustard."

"Money, money," she says, handing back change, happy to do so as long as it's small.

"Corn dog," he says, ready to eat.

"Money, money, money, money," she says.

The line is long. Business is good. But it will be better, Phyllis says to herself, as she rings up the register as if she were playing a piano.

"Money, money …"

"Give me an 'e,'" a contestant says.

Phyllis smiles. She has already guessed the whole hidden phrase. Now for the prize, she can barely wait to see what some lucky fool has won.

THE PARTICULARS OF THE RALPHS

Phyllis went to college back in 'the day' which was where she met Ralph who went to college as well for as long as his money held out. In the end, it didn't.

Ralph studied the impractical—English, Latin, philosophy, Ancient Greek. Nothing useful. No courses in business. No engineering. And he even skipped law school. He took pottery, a little music, a dash of theater—Ralph did what he enjoyed.

He joined a fraternity and waited tables there to pay his tuition and rent, and there, on a dare, he made corn dogs for the brothers. That led to corn dogs for Sunday dinner at the frat. Then he made them for other frats, then a sorority or two, then at some sports games, 'Get your corn dogs here, Ralph's Corny Doo's,' and towards the end of his college days he hosted a Corn Dog Festival and a Corn Dog Float during Homecoming Week. Somewhere along that journey Phyllis became the Corn Dog Queen (she swears she will never dress up as a corn dog again). And that's where they met, and where their history began.

The future Phyllis was not one for learning. She felt money was wasted on books she never read. And all the fraternity boys talked about were the girls from rich families.

She wasn't from one of those. She was looking for new adventures when she became the Corn Dog Queen and mistook Ralph, Corn Dog King, for a hippy. It was, after all, the Late Hippy Era. She easily seduced herself into the misadventures she might have with such a fellow.

By the time she recovered from her delusions, they were married, she was a mother, and they were living above Ralph's corn dog store. There was a pig sty out back and cornfields beyond that, and she was sleeping with a man who dreamed in Platonic dialogues.

Ugh! was her basic reaction.

Then comes the day the Money Master hops out of the television.

Ralph, of course, is a dreamer. He is ever on a quest for the Good. But Phyllis has her own dreams, and to her Ralph wastes his precious time dreaming the wrong things. And he spends way too much time thinking. He has always been more interested in words and their connections to things and how words are connected with each other. He is concerned with what others feel and what they think, too. He is dedicated to change—for himself, for this world, through reason and work.

He came home from college to work on the family farm, still seeking the Good. How one might better plow the fields. Or if it would be good to grow corn of a different color. Or if it might be good to grow his own seed and breed his own pigs rather than buy seed and pigs from the mega-corporations. Or if he should raise pigs in a way that made them more content—avoiding the thought of how pigs are slaughtered in the end.

Two weeks into his farming career, his father fired him.

"You cannot plow a field and read a book at the same time!" his father said. "And when we plow our fields, we plow them up and down; not left to right, like lines in your Plato."

Small towns being what they are, then as now, to make a living Ralph opened a restaurant which became his little corn dog store. By the time Stella was born this little corn dog shop had a growing reputation and his corn dogs became known as the food of the gods.

Meanwhile Phyllis had discovered Ralph was not the exciting happy hippy of her dreams, and she lost interest in being a happy hippy chick. She wanted the things an American should want, and Ralph was never going to make enough money to provide her with that. And so she set out—even way back then—to change Ralph.

But Ralph didn't change, and over the years Phyllis has grown increasingly unhappy. She doesn't like where they live. She doesn't like their work. She doesn't like the clothes she wears. She doesn't like the clothes he wears. She doesn't like their friends, their customers, their neighbors. She doesn't like the stuff they make—the pigs, the corn dogs, the corn. 'Pig's food,' she calls it. In the end, perhaps she just doesn't like Ralph.

Or herself. But that's part of our culture of change: new cars, new addresses, new friends, new tastes. Trying to change into something you aren't, into something you can never be—younger, thinner, richer, happy. That is to say, she had grown dissatisfied. It was time to spend money to create some sort of happiness. Throw away what fails you; buy something new.

Phyllis doesn't see that, of course. She lives on the surface, listens to television, reads ads in magazines, imagines herself somewhere other than where she is. She would say she doesn't want much, just what she deserves. Ads tell her that, and she agrees with the ads. The movies tell her that, too. What novels she reads, they are along the same line. She deserves a nice house (big), nice things (designer labels), money (lots of it), sex (or its substitute), a nice car (or two), good wine (expensive), and friends who recognize her big house, nice car, nice things, etc.

It is our birthright, isn't it? It's what we've been promised, no? Because, by god, we're American; free, white, and Republican.

"You're a Republican?" Ralph asks, somewhat surprised the first time she brings it up.

"I'm a queen," she says. "That's what I deserve. We won the war. We beat them all. We are the best. We are exceptional."

So it is that she is a fertile ground for the Master and his work.

PHYLLIS MAKES HER CASE

"A money machine," she says to Ralph. "It's on TV. Everyone's got one."

The lunch rush is over.

"Yes," Ralph says, dutifully. He is on his knees on the floor, cleaning his drips of splattered grease.

"I want to be rich," she says. "I want a money machine."

Ralph loves Phyllis dearly, despite all her faults and foibles, all their differences in thought. After all, she has bore him his beloved daughter, Stella, the only person on earth who he feels understands him and shares his loves for thinking, philosophy, and corn dogs.

Ralph steals a few glances at his Plato, open to a passage on Value. He wishes he could discover Plato's—or Socrates'—notions on business, wealth, cash, or commerce. Are these categories of the Good? What is the nature of wealth, of money? How did those philosophers live in a world apparently without such things? Or did they simply not bother with such pettiness? He finds no answers there.

Phyllis does her best thinking when counting receipts at the end of the rush. But today she is obsessed with the Money Master's offer to teach Ralph the nature of getting on in the business world. So many possibilities, she thinks, if Ralph would only stop thinking so much.

She tabulates today's sales, compares them to yesterday's, and this week to last week, and this month to the same month last year, pondering what to expect from tomorrow, will it be good, or bad, where they are headed, and what can they do to get richer and richer, to accumulate more and more.

Not to mention determining today's return on investment, sales and costs, cost per sales, food sold, paper goods consumed, today's share of utilities, rent, wear and tear on equipment. And salaries—ugh. Then net income from operations emerges at the bottom of the list, how lovely. Before taxes. Ugh!

"Ralph!" she says. "You're reading too much. You should be thinking about how to make a better corn dog, how to cut costs, how to raise prices, how to expand into the world market …"

"Oh, turtledove, I will do better," he says. Debating her will only lead to another argument. So Ralph agrees. Ralph always agrees. They rarely argue.

She cuts him off.

"No, Ralph," she says. "It's time for you to restructure the corn dog business."

She opens her ledger.

"Plato never sold a corn dog in his life," she says. "We need a bigger business, more customers, more profits. We need to grow. We need to make money. We need a bigger store. We need a warehouse to distribute. We need outlets. Walmart. Amazon. Best Buy. Costco. We need a web presence. We need a feedlot and more pigs in it. Bigger pigs. Real porkers."

Ralph smiles. He is on his knees, scrubbing the floor. Phyllis taps her foot close to his face.

"I want to be someone of means, Ralph. I want to be somebody. I want class. Untie that silly apron, take off that silly hat, and—God, you look like such a Democrat—get ready to go study at the Dollartorium."

She puts the cash in a deposit bag and turns to her books. A chart over her desk shows sales up and down, rates of change, cash in and deposits.

"Your days of raising hogs are over."

"I like my hogs," Ralph says. "Although I'm sorry we have to slaughter them in the end, the little dears. Still, we need to make the wieners."

Phyllis opens her ledger and adds numbers to the columns, totals them up, adds dates, sums and fractions, ratios and percentages. She knits her brows and points to the chart on the wall.

"Business, Ralph. Business."

She points to the lines—the black ones, the red ones—on the chart.

"That's what it's about."

"Oh."

"It's time we move on, out of the drab middle class."

"I didn't know we had moved in," he says. "And if we do, what happens to all our hogs and corn?"

She scoots back and stands up, then looks Ralph straight in the face.

"Have you ever heard of the Dollartorium?" she asks.

Ralph is worried he's about to be scolded. He rolls the

bucket around by the mop. He rolls it around now so it is between him and her. Then, it's under the table and under the chairs. Every day there is mopping to do when the lunch rush is over and the store is closed.

"Have I heard about the what, Angel Puss?" Ralph asks.

"You're going there. You're going to the Dollartorium."

"Never heard of it," he says. "Must I?"

"I've made an appointment for you. Go pick up a machine and learn how to run it. That is to say, you need to learn how we can get rich."

Now Ralph is worried because, whatever it is, whatever she wants, it does not sound like it's for the Good. But he loves her. He does. He wonders what would Plato do, what would Socrates say about it?

But Ralph knows he has lost the argument, if it was an argument.

THE MORNING AFTER

Next morning the sun comes up as Ralph wakes from his troubled dreams. He hears the television on downstairs; odd, because the store is closed, and Phyllis still lies beside him snoring. As he dresses, Ralph recalls his dreams of the Dollartorium and what his Phyllis has been insisting that he do.

"I don't suppose Plato would object to me picking up a few drachmas," Ralph says to himself.

He flips on the lights and puts on work clothes.

"I wouldn't mind a few extra dollars myself. I need a new bookshelf. And there are some books I'd like to get."

He goes downstairs to the Doggery.

"I could donate to the food bank, too, if I were rich," he mumbles to himself. "No one should be hungry in this day and place."

"Ralph, Ralph, Ralph, Ralph, Ralph, Ralph, Ralph," a voice says. It comes from the TV high on the wall.

"Who are you?" Ralph asks.

"Who am I? Who are you?" the voice says. "Who is anyone?"

The store is empty. The doors are locked.

"We've got business to discuss," the man says. He jumps from the TV to the counter.

"We're closed," Ralph says.

What is happening is quite impossible, Ralph thinks. He does not talk to television sets. To Plato, Socrates, Alcibiades, Meno, yes. But not to a television or to characters who leap from them.

"You have been chosen," the man says. The man is short and sprightly.

"Chosen?" Ralph asks. "I'm too busy to be chosen for anything."

The Money Master—cane in hand—leaps to the floor. It is the Money Master, indeed.

"Voila," he says. "I am here, and you are chosen. Your tuition is paid in full."

The Money Master wears his normal red, white, and blue, all spangles and glitters, feathered in dollars from boots to hat. Upbeat music, catchy, clever Broadway tunes flow from the television. Now Ralph feels like he should have a cane, as well, something to twirl. He feels he should put on a hat, doff it, and follow the Master in a parade around the room. The Master has that effect.

"Hello, sweetheart," he says to Ralph. "I am the Money Master."

"We're closed," Ralph says. "We haven't made our corn dogs yet. Come back tomorrow."

Too strange, perhaps, how the Money Master moves about, a paradox—like particles and waves that have come through the television. Well, why not? Who's to say those beings inside televisions don't look out at us and wonder how we in 'the real' endure with all our clumsiness, without sponsors, and last for a mere one season with no possibility of reruns.

The Money Master has come to fetch poor Ralph.

"Today you come to me," the Money Master says. "To study at the Dollartorium. Phyllis has prepped you for your studies, I hope."

"I have to work today," Ralph says. "Maybe later."

"Ralph, Ralph," the Money Master says. "Work is for others. Especially for you to do such minimum wage stuff. You should be on the beach, by a pool, drinking wine, your arms around some half-naked woman.

"Is that working?"

"Or at a casino, gambling, winning!—or losing—not caring because we have made you rich—and you laugh, and drink. Or you are ten floors up above the stinking city sitting in your office, deciding the fate of others, those who have served you well or not, those who have been loyal, punishing others who've not, or who've failed you, deciding who lives, who dies, that sort of thing, and getting richer despite all your losses."

He pokes his cane into Ralph's chest.

"Ralph, my man," he says, "you are to come study at the Dollartorium. You've secured a seat there. Your Phyllis has signed you up and paid your fees. Congratulations."

He holds Ralph's hand as he pulls back and forth, strutting, spinning his cane like a baton, getting closer and closer to the television set. Ralph wonders if he will be pulled into it. Then what?

"I'm offering you a path that millions can only dream of

taking. The American dream. I offer what all Americans are promised the day we are born. To be someone your wife can be proud of."

The Money Master stops again, gets close again, cuddles up, whispers in Ralph's ear.

"She paid the bribe. You are in. It's non-refundable."

Then the Money Master is on the counter again, dancing, tapping his cane, strutting about, singing: "Money, money, money, money. Money is the thing of dreams …"

"Why me?"

"Why not?" the Master asks.

"I don't need to be rich," Ralph says. "Comfortable is fine. I'm comfortable."

"Comfortable!" the Money Master says. He faces Ralph. "Dipping and selling corn dogs? Grinding and stuffing pork? On your feet all day? Killing hogs? Picking corn? Too much work, Ralph!" The Money Master whispers in Ralph's ear. "It's time to cash in. Everyone does it who can. It's all the rage."

The Money Master stops in the center of the room, arms akimbo.

"Your finances are in the shit house, Ralph. Your future is a cold corn dog. No, Ralph, it's time to learn business. How to deal. How to make deals. How to break deals. How to make deals on wheels. How to wheedle and deedle, and pile up the profits, so you can make better deals, bigger deals, more deals, bigger piles."

He pauses. Ralph leans on his counter and stares at the Master.

"Ralph, Ralph, Ralph," the Master says. "Money's where the money's at. You won't have to work. It's easy-peasy. Make up your mind," the Master says, tapping his head. "Because I have to go. Many are wanting in. Few will be admitted."

The Money Master leaps up to the counter and near the television, which he turns on, ready to leap back in and go home.

"Well, I don't mind working," Ralph says.

The Master hands Ralph brochures and a map. Ralph looks through them, the regular promises and puffery. But Ralph is mild-mannered. He tries to be kind. It's the only way he knows how to be. Not how to brag. Nor to lie. Nor how to fake it. Nor make excuses. And he also does not want to break his poor Phyllis's heart. Has she been disappointed in him? He loves her, God help him, and he wonders if he should change, because being rich would be a mighty big change.

Ralph is what he is, and he feels comfortable as himself, perhaps too old to become somebody other than what he is. And change involves so much work. Perhaps he's done too much thinking, studied too much philosophy. Perhaps he has ignored his wife. Perhaps he should investigate this Dollartorium thing. He doesn't have to buy into it or change too much. But then he also might learn something new, and that's a good thing, isn't it? How bad can a bad thing be? How wrong can a bad thing make a good man go wrong?

He's that naïve.

"Well, maybe I could go for a little while. See what they do. See how they do it. What can go wrong with just looking?"

"Good man," says the Master. He leaps up on the counter. "We'll expect you today. You've made a wise choice.

Or at least your wife did. And at least you obey her. I've thrown in full coverage, insurance if things go wrong. Just a few dollars more. Not that things ever go wrong. But if they do by some remarkable fate, you'll get a discount on the very next course."

With a leap and a twirl, the Money Master leaps to the set, then inside, then off. The screen shrinks to a dot. And then there is nothing. No, nothing. No, nothing at all.

THE MASTER IS CHANNELED

Now for a few words about the Money Master. We have seen him in action, how he jumps about, in and out of TVs and into our lives, how he dances on countertops, that sort of thing.

He's a narrow little fellow—an ancient gnome theory goes—who wraps himself in money and spangles, and often in the American flag, and who has bought time on television so he can teach others how he has grown so rich, so they can do likewise. Who doesn't want to be just like him?

But why is he teaching us schmucks how to get rich? What's in it for him? Why doesn't the Money Master choose an easier path and spend his days just being rich—in the sun on a beach, all desires being answered? Flaunting wealth in his mansion, tipping the servants? 'Oh, thank you. Thank you, Mr. Master,' they will say, and bow, and back away. Endowing charities and arts at fashionable balls for the poor and creative? Wear a silly suit of dollar bills, that shed money?

Something is missing if we think dollars are the highest Good. There's power which might fill the hollowness in the Master' heart. A hole. A chamber of nothing. And even a rich man needs to feel something. Needs to be loved. Needs the applause. A bit of a need to feel like a god, and a bit of a need to have others agree. Because money, just money is never enough. Power over others, adulation, and fame, and the glory of worship. Money is power, but that's how that power is used.

The Money Master doesn't admit this. He never admits anything. He would certainly never admit to a weakness.

Greed is his engine. Power is its own system of logic, its own world, its own rules. His beauty is glitter. To morph greed into power, into absolute power, into power over others, into control overall, at least over those who adore him the most. His fans. His sycophants. To be served in his kingdom.

Now he wants Ralph in his legion.

You see that in his TV ads. He wants to draw Ralph to the Dollartorium. He wants to train him to be his sycophant.

The Dollartorium is not a school, nor a place, nor a house; not a kingdom, nor a state, nothing like Mar-a-Lago. Well, maybe a little bit like Mar-a-Lago. It is not a corporation. More than a string of golf courses. More than a resort. Not a private island. It is more than we outsiders see—more than any dream we poor may dream. More than any delusions we deluded create. The Dollartorium is in fact just a dirty little factory that sits where they are barely noticed—one of many such factories teaching the wealthy here and there—some buried in the wilderness, some in cities, some in some forlorn countries, a few buried deep in the ground, all of which are where darkness is light, where evil is good, where truth is a lie. Where, if you ask any question, the answer is cash.

Only the invited can enter a Dollartorium. You must want to go. The tuition is high. Inside the place might seem modest, a small, dingy place, under the influence of the

Master. Like a mirror, or a dream. But it becomes, not what one sees, but what one wants, our invisible desires. Fantasies. Luxuries. Where anything is possible, even the ridiculous. Especially the ridiculous.

Such is the magic of the Money Masters everywhere, and their creations.

The Master here flies about the place—and from here to there, and back again, from one media event to another—on his hot air balloon. He floats above the earth. He avoids walking on the ground. He comes into your homes on late night tv.

The road, or path, or trail to his Dollartorium is dangerous, too. Our wayfaring Ralph has a map and directions to go this way and that, go left and go right, go up and go down, go here and go there, avoid this trap, this tree, that leopard, that sink hole, this lender, that credit card, this scam, vote left, vote right, lie a lot, etc., etc., all of which are traps that litter the treacherous path to the Dollartorium. No one would dare go there if not for the empty promises that inhabit many souls that yearn to be filled. Or on the insistence of others who insist, and insist, and at last—to find peace—one seeks to find what can possibly lie beyond the Good that comes natural.

Long ago gnomes lived in the earth and made gold and gems and protected their wealth by burying their treasures. They were ugly short little things, or so we've been told, little hands, little mouths, tufts of hair, and a cynical attitude. Good people avoided the gnomes. But from time to time, one could not help but encounter them. They had most of the money, after all.

And gnomes created these Dollartoriums. The gnomes

ventured out to enrich their riches, or to get elected, or to capture more servants, or to get on TV. That sort of thing. The Money Master is a modern version of them. You can sometimes espy others playing golf. Or sitting front and center in the most expensive seats at the theater. But it is easier to find them if you know where they are.

These gnomes come disguised. Otherwise, who would suffer such monsters to live at all, such wretches spreading their wretchedness about. If things were normal, they would be driven out of town. Once you know how they do what they do, you can spot them, their shifty looks and sinister smiles, their misdeeds, how they walk, or slide along, or brag, wah-wah-wah, while talking only about themselves, all good things reduced to cash in one form or another, creating safety for themselves by sewing fear everywhere.

Such arts are taught at the Dollartorium. Some students catch on quickly. Especially those born with the skills for untruth, or have silver spoons in their mouths. For them, the country clubs exist, the private clubs, and the fraternities, of course. Secret societies. Religious sects. Voodoo cults. Political parties. Others never learn to use the tricks well and thus are forever condemned to serve the rich in the hopes they'll someday be like them.

From time to time, a few, like Ralph are called to learn and serve. The lucky, the new, are invited into the Dollartorium to refresh the ruling class. The Money Master reigns over many.

"Hey, little man," the Master says on TV. "Are you tired? Are you broke? Have you been shit on at work? Been pushed out of your job? Turned down for a raise? Follow me, follow me."

Through ads like this the Master gathers his mob, those who want to be rich like the Master is rich, who are naturally brash, who want the women he gets, who want to live in his house, who want to be in his tribe, who want to join his club, who want to kiss where he walks, who want to kiss where he sits, who want to broadcast his lies, who want to think like he thinks—if what he thinks is really thinking at all.

That said, who knows otherwise why he is what he is? He is probably lonely. He is certainly unloved, even if worshipped by those caught in his trap. And all of this is his way of acting out pain. He is a danger to us, a dangerous human, if he is indeed human. The jury is out.

Poor Ralph knows nothing of any of this. He is just curious and in love with his wife. He'd like her to be happy, or he would stay at home and dip dogs.

STELLA ARGUES OTHERWISE

The pigs are kept out back. You come to town, you drive down Main, you see the Corny Doo Doggery there, and above the store is Ralph's apartment. You can't see it from Main Street but their garden is out back, and then there's a fence, and then the pigsty. The pigs are wallowing in the mud. Behind that the creek, and across that, corn fields. Beyond that, the hills rise up, and beyond that, pastures, and fences, and Kansas, and all the rest of America.

Stella is feeding the pigs. She collects slops from around town, and from the Doggery, of course—old vegetables, stale cornbread, uneaten lunches, mixed with pig chow. They have half a dozen hogs and some of the hogs have piglets too young to know their bleak future. For the moment the pigs are quite happy, rooting through slops or running free, squealing and pushing each other through mud as they await a turn to suckle.

Stella wears her rubber boots, one on the ground, one on a rail to steady herself as she stands in the mud. Farms are messy. Especially pig farms. And they smell, more so as things warm up in the afternoon. But that suits pigs just fine. Stella hoses them down which cools them off and keeps off the flies.

"Sweet Stella," Ralph says. He carries his book as he

saunters out back. A finger holds his place in the book. He always keeps his philosophy book near by, for in his mind, there is always an argument to be discussed.

"Why so sad, Daddy?" Stella asks, hand on her hip as stands with the pigs.

"I sometimes wish I was as happy as these hogs," Ralph says. "All they do is eat slop and roll in mud. If all I had to do was to make corn dogs and read Plato, I'd be happy, too. But I have to please your mother."

Stella sighs. "What is she saying now?"

"She met a man on television."

"Oh, dear," Stella says. "Someday she'll get you on one of her game shows."

"She's been taken in by an infomercial."

"Television," Stella says with a huff. "It's one long advertisement, getting you to buy what you don't need, to make you think you don't have enough, or you don't have the right thing, or you're too small, and too weak, and too poor, and too scared, or that you smell funny. We ought to get rid of television."

"I don't think that will ever happen," Ralph says.

"Mother's so unhappy," Stella says.

"She listened to this fella on television who has a machine for getting rich. Now she wants us to buy one and then have me learn how to run it."

Stella squirts a sow in the eye, washing mud off its face. The sow squeals. But it is pleased.

"I wish Plato wrote about business," Ralph says. "What it is. How to do it. What is right and wrong when it comes to money. Plato is so good with Virtue, on the Good, on Poetics, on Politics, but not one word on advertising or the media. I don't think Plato ever ran a real business."

Ralph has his foot up on the fence as he watches his pigs.

You get used to the smell. If you're away for a long time, you can miss it.

"There must have been rich Greeks, Daddy," Stella says. Slops sound just like slops as she pours another bucket of them into the trough.

"But they didn't have television," Ralph says.

"If people mind their own business, they don't have time for television. People who live in the moment and have real work to do are happier than those who can't get away from the thing."

Ralph loves Stella. She is more than his daughter. She is also his loving companion. Her voice is like his, her thoughts are his thoughts made fresh. He approves of her and trusts her opinions, something he needs—don't we all—in a world of fakery.

"Greed," Stella says. She shakes her head. She needs say no more. They've often had this conversation.

The sow rolls over in the mud, belly side up. Stella hoses off the mud, cleaning the table for those piggies too young for the slops. They rush to the mother sow, eager for lunch.

"No one in America thinks a poor man is good," Ralph says. His thoughts trail off. "Maybe I've read too many books." He pauses. "Or the wrong ones."

With the tip of her boot, Stella nudges the piglets, and they squeal, butt heads, fight for teats. Momma sow grunts and rolls to her other side. Stella hoses that side off, and the piglets belly up, sliding in and around each other, struggling for their place at the table.

Watching animals eat, watching the sun in the sky, such is the best part of life on the farm. Things just grow, the sun just shines. There's not much one has to do to make that happen. It just happens. You get out of the way. You plant seeds, it rains, corn grows. Soon you've got a harvest. Corn, and hogs, and corn dogs, all come along so naturally.

"I hate the rich, Daddy," Stella says.

She pauses, then sighs.

"They make a person feel poor. And they make us think poor is bad. All pigs need are mud and slops. All our corn needs is a little bit of rain and some sunshine."

Stella turns off the hose, the water stops, and the piglets finish fighting for lunch.

It's a warm summer day, mid-morning, and there is an invasion of black flies. The flies eat manure, then birds eat the flies, then cats eat the birds, then pigs eat the cats, and we all know those fat pigs and ground ripe corn are just one short step to a delicious corn dog. Which we then eat.

Stella is young and lovely, a woman of excellent proportions—not too thin as is too much the fashion, but strong and of the earth in a way that seems serene, with a lovely way of looking plain, accepting things around her, like her father always lost in philosophy, but taking it from nature and not from books. Like her mother Stella longs for something of a quiet life, not only for herself, but for all of us. Stella weathers the changes that come her way, wrestling with forces without using force, connecting what otherwise seems so disconnected. She sees the whole as well as the individuals that create it. They are standing in the field of green corn taller than they are. The moment is effortless.

Ralph kicks a clod, his favorite way to express himself.

"Corn's coming along good."

"Happy up to the day we chop it down and grind its seeds."

"The pigs seem happy, too," Ralph says.

"Yep," Stella says. "Happy right up to the day we turn them into sausage."

RALPH DEBATES WITH HIMSELF

Now it is tomorrow. The lunch rush has started, the doors are open, customers are coming in, and Ralph finds himself dipping and wrapping, dipping and wrapping, handing off corndogs, one after another. Then another. And another.

But Ralph isn't there, not really there, but somewhere lost in thought. He doesn't smile. He doesn't greet the customers, not even his regulars, not even his friends. He is involved with a dialogue deep in his mind. Not with Plato, not with Socrates, but with himself. Should he go to the Dollartorium? Should he change his life? What is money? What is important? What is the Good?

He may well be the loneliest person on the planet. Even though he is working, even though there are customers, even though the shop is busy, and he is cooking, wrapping, dipping, smiling—and thinking, he feels very much alone. He thinks out loud, as if he is talking to his customers, but they are used to Ralph doing that, even as he talks to phantoms in the air.

"As far as I can tell," Ralph says, "the rich are getting richer, and the poor are getting ... what? screwed? That Money Master wasn't wrong there. If I think about it much, my own economics, the situation I'm in, the way the money comes out at the end of the month—and it mostly goes out—that's how I get rated by other folks …" He pauses. "Or do they even bother rating me at all? That can't be good. I suspect they rate others on the amount of goods and cash they have, houses, how many bathrooms, addresses, cars, pools, clothes. If so, I fear I'm at the bottom of the heap. But don't we all suffer from the same thing? Even some of our customers see me as a poor, working stiff on the far side of the counter. Cooking for you. Waiting for you. Picking up your trash. Thinking I'm poor. Dirt poor. Hog farm poor. And maybe I am, and getting poorer because everyone else, on the news, on the television, in the papers, is getting rich, or says they are. I'm falling behind. Not that I'm not working, or that my work is not good," he thinks. "My work is good, the finest corn dogs in the world, and I love making them. But good work means less and less to other folks these days. What you can count is all that counts anymore. And you are ranked by how big a heap of it you've gotten."

He dips another rack of corndogs in the grease and watches as they sizzle in the hog grease. He loves his corn dogs. He's proud of them. People want them, enjoy them, and eat them often.

He lifts them out, they're done, and he lets the grease drip free, then hangs them up to sell.

"Perhaps I need a plan," Ralph thinks. "What is that money machine all about? And what about this Dollartorium? Mr. Plato, how do things work in this modern world where Greece is just a beach where the rich go to sun themselves, a destination for their cruise ships, a place to moor their yachts? How does this money mind change philosophy? I guess old Plato never made much cash. What was there to invest in anyway? How rich did Socrates have to be to have a porch stoop for an office? He probably didn't even own a decent pair of Italian shoes. Maybe everything he said was meant in irony. Or did he say it all just to make trouble for the city and the gods?"

"I'll have a corn dog," a customer says.

"And where did that get you, Mr. Socrates?"

Ralph picks the corn dog from the rack, wraps it in paper, then hands it to the customer.

"Good afternoon, Mrs. Frost."

But he doesn't mean it. Today he just mimics his interest, pretending he is there and has a customer.

"Good afternoon, Mr. Cummings," Ralph says. "Enjoy the dog." But to himself he's asking, 'Have I missed how things really work and are not just shadows on the wall?'

He bends down to face a little girl who is getting her first corndog.

"Now, here's a special Corny Doo for you, my little friend," he says.

She takes a bite and smiles at the man who has made her happy.

'Things are not 'things,' now, are they, Mr. Plato?' Ralph is thinking. 'I'm getting it now. Things are only Things. Forms are perfect. Got it now. Like shapes. Like numbers. Yes. Got it. So, what's Good is that which never changes, is that which is eternal, immutable, like numbers, math. Got it. A corn dog is a corn dog, and corn dogs can be eaten, but Money is a Form, and Forms are what's Real, they never change and last forever. Money is forever.'

Ralph almost burns himself with dripping grease. He stares into space, stares into the emptiness of the television set on the wall above the register. The nothingness, the noise, the clowns, the laughter. The line of customers has halted in front of him. Oops. Pay attention, Ralph tells himself.

"Then, if that's so," Ralph says out loud, "then Money is the eternal Good."

"Can I have extra mustard?" a customer asks.

Ralph looks him in the eye—a rotund man who wears a tie and must have come from some nearby office for lunch. He hands him a fresh corndog, repeating the word. "Money."

"Thank you," the customer says. Then he holds up two fingers. "I'd like two today, if you don't mind."

Ralph gives him another without thinking. The man holds out his dollars. Ralph stares at the customer, but indicates it is Phyllis who takes the cash.

"You pay up front to the woman who has always known what money is."

Phyllis frowns, no doubt thinking her mantra, 'Time is money.' "Let the line move along now, Ralph," Phyllis says, politely grimacing at this interruption in the flow of things.

"Corn dogs," Ralph says to himself. "Who cares about corn dogs? Nobody. Not Plato. Not the rich. Not …" He hesitates as he thinks through this new truth. "Not me. Mutable. Fickle. Bound to grow old, mold, become food for the rats. Not a Form. Not at all."

He looks up to see a customer waiting to be served.

"I've worked all my life and got nothing," Ralph says.

"Corn dog, please."

Another customer.

"Corn dog."

"All my life, I've been such a fool. All my pockets have always been empty," he says. "My pockets, look, empty. Corn dogs are just so much cold gruel. In fact…"

"Two corn dogs," the next customer says. "Extra mustard."

"Two corn dogs. Mustard's at the register."

But Ralph's eyes are glassy, his work mechanical.

"All my life I've been shit on, shoved this way and that, spit on and fired, and look where I'm at. I'm a doormat," he says. "Making corn dogs for others. A tool for their pleasure."

He catches a stare from a customer who maybe hears him, maybe doesn't, certainly doesn't understand. He hands her a corn dog wrapped in paper.

"Come to think of it," Ralph says. "I've been walked on, run over, now I've got marks up my back. I'm a doormat," he says, "who rich people scorn, while I make them all corn dogs. What's the point in all that?"

"Do you have fries?"

"For fries, go to McDonalds."

His mood has turned dark. For the rest of the rush Ralph works in oblivion, but slowly, quite slowly he begins to count. How many customers does he have? How many dogs is he selling? How much per dog is profit? How much do the ingredients cost? How much money is in the till? How much more money is there than yesterday? Or less? How much will be left over at the end of the day? Will the day be good now that what's good is cash?

It is interesting, but not joyous.

He needs a vacation. How much would that cost? How old is his car? How awkward is it that he lives over the shop? Not even a house. Not even a yard. Who is this Ralph who wears a paper hat, wears an apron stained with grease and cornmeal, who spends his day serving fools? What does it all mean? What if he dies? How much will that cost? Do they have enough money in the bank? Does anything mean anything anymore?

He makes up his mind. He will go to the Dollartorium. What can go wrong? We'll have to see.

"Daddy, daddy, wake up, lunch is over," Stella says, bringing Ralph back to the moment. "It's time to clean up the Doggery."

Part 2

THE DOLLARTORIUM

In the middle of the journey of his life Ralph finds himself lost as he follows the route to the Dollartorium. Although an 'x' marks the location of the Dollartorium, his map seems to have led him nowhere so far. For a moment it appears to be a short distance from the river, over the next few rolling hills, across a stretch of blue grass prairie, then down a creek, then up another, and so on, and so on, but he never gets to where he's going.

The way splits, and Ralph chooses one path that later merges with another until he reaches the top of a hill, but from there he can only see more endless grass stretching before him, no different than the grass he has been walking through all day. It simply goes on. Just more rounded hills, another gully, another valley, until—well, Ralph is lost.

From time-to-time Ralph follows the map through a small town, but there is no one in the place, only rutted roads and dilapidated buildings, worthless ruins, as if all the life and energy has been sucked out of these places. All is silent out here except for the steady wind. He passes abandoned farms, rusted riderless tractors sitting motionless in the fields. The further he goes, the bleaker it is. What will it be like there, he wonders, as he draws closer and closer to the Dollartorium.

At last, he comes upon a sign, 'Dollartorium Just Ahead.'

"Ah, well," Ralph says to himself. "If I haven't been going the right way so far, at least I haven't gone the wrong one."

More signs. 'Take a Right.' 'Keep Right.' 'No left turn.' Or, 'Dollartorium, One Way.' 'No U-turn.' 'No Exit.' And, finally, 'The Dollartorium. You are Here.'

"Oh," Ralph says. He is in a gully overgrown with shrubs and trees, away from the wind, a dark and foreboding place. It has been a long trip and now it is late afternoon. He confronts a heavy wooden door with a small window which blocks his way forward. Walls reach out on both sides as far as Ralph can see, making the gully he is in impassable. He can either knock or go back home.

He knocks. He is here, after all.

Then he notices the sign: "If you knock, we don't hear you. If you're in, get out. If you think you're expected, you're not."

Daunting.

He knocks again on a large, gilded knocker. It creates a deep hollow sound as if all is empty behind the door.

"Who's there?" a voice asks behind the door. It sounds far away. "Who's knocking? Go away. There's no one here."

Ralph stretches on tiptoes to try and see in, but the window is too high.

"My name is Ralph," he says.

"Ralph, Ralph, Ralph. Yes, well, no, we've never heard of you. You're not on my list. So, you can't be here."

"But I am here," Ralph says.

"Not to us. You're not on my list, and you're not inside,

and you never will be. So, you can't come in. We have too many applicants already. What a mess. And the new ones are so much work. There are too many in here now, so there will not be enough of what little we have for me. So, sorry. Go home."

Perhaps, Ralph thinks, he is talking into some sort of microphone and speaker device. He sees no one, nor any device that might connect him to the inside. He knocks again.

"If you're here begging, we don't have any money," the voice says.

A pause. He knocks again.

"If you are running for office, I already voted."

Pause. He knocks again.

"If you want to save me from damnation, I'd rather be damned."

Pause.

Ralph has the ticket Phyllis got for him. And he is afraid to go back and face her, his wife, if he fails to get in. He checks the sign. Yes, it says 'Dollartorium.' He checks his ticket. It also says 'Dollartorium.' He checks the date. Yes, today is today and not some other time. So, he is where and when he should be. He can't imagine there are two such places. And even if he should leave, where would he go? It's a long way back. It's growing dark. And he's come this far. Furthermore, if he could admit such a thing to himself, he would admit he is lost.

Ralph tries to be polite. "Please let me in," he says. "I'm here to see someone. I have a ticket. If you open the door, I'll explain."

"What ticket? Show me."

The door opens a crack. Ralph passes the ticket through.

"Who sold you this?" the voice asks. "We're busy in here. I'm busy in here. I have no time for this incessant knocking. I'm allergic to knocking and loud noises. You'll wake my dog. I'm not feeling well. You're at the wrong place. So, stop all this. Stop it! Stop it! I have something on the stove. Don't wake the baby. My husband's coming and he shouldn't see us together."

Ralph hesitates to name what it is that he sees through the crack in the door. It doesn't look human. It's a creature of some sort. Half snake, perhaps, half lizard, little more than four feet tall, and, although walking on two legs like a human, with two hands with the tiniest, skinniest fingers, it also seems to scurry about on four legs. Still, there is something human about it.

"Hello," Ralph says. "I've come a long way to pick up a money machine my wife has bought. And someone here is supposed to give me lessons on how to run it."

"Machine, machine, machine," the creature says. "Money, money, money. So, you call yourself a customer. And you pretend to be a student. So you say you have a ticket. So you pretend we owe you lessons. Well, classes are closed, the semester is starting, the machines are sold out, I'm expecting someone else, I don't have time for you or your nonsense, you're possibly contagious, and I don't like you anyway. So sorry. No, I'm not. Goodbye."

"But the man on television, you know, with the hat …"

"With the hat? Not the Master … ?" The creature's voice hints of awe. Even reverence. The door opens a bit.

"Well, I think so, I don't know, he talked to me, but my

wife is the one who bought the machine. This man sold her that ticket. Then she sent me here. Phyllis. Maybe it's her name on the list. I could go home. I just want my machine. And an instruction manual."

Suddenly the door opens completely.

"Oh, Phyllis! The beautiful Phyllis. Phyllis who manages the Corny Doo empire."

Then Ralph is quickly pulled in by his apron, and the door shuts behind him.

"I'm Ralph," Ralph says. "She manages me. I do what I can to manage the Corny Doo Doggery."

At last, he is where he's been going. He sighs. He's tired.

How different it is inside. As light slowly grows brighter his eyes adjust to the difference. He sees marble walls, marble floors, chrome fixtures, mirrors, gold, and glitter—lots of glitter—with which the place is decorated. It is a huge space, vacuous, well-lit, and nothing at all like the dark prairie outside through which he has been trekking, with its ruined towns and abandoned farms. Clean, empty, well-lit, sterile, cold. Ceilings so high it is hard to see where they end. Floors so shiny it is hard not to slip, and when you look down it's like you look into hell. But it's only a reflection of the heavens.

For all the world, Ralph fears he is in the lobby of some grand hotel in some expensive city, certainly a place more expensive than anywhere he can afford to stay, in a place such as he has only read about, or seen on television, a place he has never been. Wherever he is, and whyever he is there, he clearly feels he doesn't belong. Not with an apron around his waist, a paper hat on his head, flour-encrusted shoes on his feet— clothes only working people wear, and no one who deserves to be in such elegance would dress so common.

"Follow me," the creature says, and it waves Ralph to follow it down a gilded way and up an escalator. Such a smooth and easy ride, Ralph thinks. But how does he get out later, he wonders. It's odd, he thinks, as he turns back to see where he's come from, ever mindful he might need to get out. There are many ways in, but he sees no exits. He senses danger.

RECEPTION

The creature leads Ralph into a massive rotunda with a high dome, the underside of which is painted with a mural—is it of the Master?—flying in the clouds, lying in his basket, his hand stretched out to another figure painted on the other side of the dome who Ralph thinks looks like himself—isn't that odd?. Thus, the painting of the Master is reaching out to Ralph, handing him a fist full of dollars. Or is he reaching out and has taken the cash. It must be done with mirrors, Ralph thinks. This is a vision of heaven as seen from inside the Dollartorium.

Here below, the creature tugs Ralph's apron as it pulls him onward, inward, deeper into the complex. Soon they arrive at another huge room at the center of which is a large pool filled with clear water. Beautiful young women are at play, swimming about, laughing, half-clad, all blonde, all white, all with makeup and smiles and thick lips, wet clothes clinging to their litheness. Who has time for this sort of thing, he wonders, but there they are. Fountains burble as the pool is fed with water, and the women splash and gently laugh to each other. This must be happiness.

Alcoves line the edges of this rotunda. Each alcove is accoutered with red leather chairs and gilded tables, gold-framed mirrors that hang from the walls, and life-sized paintings of the Master—the Master on a horse, the Master half naked, the Master clutching dollars, or the Master stretched seductively across a bed. Magazine covers have been framed and hung on the walls, from movie magazines, news magazines, financial journals, and newspapers—all of them featuring the Master. The Master posing with famous men. The Master posing with beautiful women. The Master as a knight in shining armor.

"He must be very famous," Ralph says.

"He is," the creature says. "He's on television."

"Then I am where I'm supposed to be," Ralph says.

"You are where you are, as you always will be," the creature says. "It's not possible to be anywhere else."

"However, one might wish otherwise," Ralph says.

Whatever it is, whoever it is, this creature is leading Ralph through gilded corridors, keeping its head down, furtively looking left and right, then looking right to left, smelling this way and that, sometimes walking on two legs, sometimes falling to all four. Ralph worries he should be worried. Marble columns. Brass doors are all shut as if to keep mysteries behind them contained and unavailable. Then more pools, more statues, more women, more paintings, all of the Master. And behind these walls and doors Ralph hears the cranking of machinery, whirring, pumping, grinding, clatter. From time-to-time he hears a scream—is it human? or a machine running out of grease?—but he dares not ask. Perhaps, Ralph thinks, some things are best left unknown.

Ralph stumbles on, following this thing. Occasionally the creature pauses, spins around, circles Ralph from left to right, smells his pant legs, smells his apron, touches his paper hat, wipes his finger on his shoes, then circles back the other way from right to left, bent low. He worries the creature might abandon him in this enormous expanse. What would he do? What direction would he go? Should he go on, or go back home? And if he wants to go home, what is the way? And failing here, what would he tell his dear Phyllis? What would he tell himself? Yet, he is certain he does not belong here.

Yes, he is intimidated.

'Do I deserve to be here?' Ralph asks himself. 'Am I worthy of such luxury? Have I earned the right to be here? Is it right for anyone to be here? Does anyone deserve this much? Why do they have as much as they have? Why don't some have as much as others? Would I dare sit on these cushy chairs? Does my butt deserve such opulence? And what makes those who are here feel they belong? What kind of people don't belong, and is that who I am? Or not?'

He is afraid to touch anything—break it, you buy it—or even to walk on the red carpets lest he leave his footprints in flour.

But his questions have no answers. He does not speak. He does not dare.

Up another escalator they go, and finally the creature leads Ralph into an interior room as spacious and lavish as any Ralph has ever seen. If this is a hotel, Ralph thinks, he could never sleep in any of its rooms, not at these prices. Or get comfortable. This is too posh to stay in, too expensive to sleep in, too overwhelming to lounge about reading Plato.

"Where are we?" he asks. "Where are we going?"

"A secret place," the creature says. "The internal place. The special place inside this very special place. You are fortunate to have been invited here. Not everyone gets a ticket. And you shouldn't ask so many questions. You shouldn't show any weakness. I'm tired of all your whining. I hope you have money for a tip."

Finally, they come to a counter in a reception area, and the creature rings a bell, ding! ding! then it hurries to the other side, puts on a cap, a short-waisted jacket, looks up and smiles at Ralph, a smile that stretches from ear to ear. Are those ears, or merely bumps on his head?

"What can I do for you?" it asks Ralph. Or she. Or he.

There are other guests whom Ralph assumes are guests, some standing in lines, some just lounging about on chairs, or leaning against pillars as they wait—for what, one wonders? Many carry their baggage. Little bags. Leather bags. Fashion bags. Duffle bags. Bags of money. Tennis bags. Golf bags. Who knows? Most are dressed quite well, in expensive suits, or dresses, with jewels, the men in shoes with pointy toes, women in high heels which make it difficult for them to walk. Or escape. But no one is walking. No one is escaping. No one is going anywhere. They stand and wait, slouching against the pillars. Or lean more than slouch; or pose more than lean; as if at any minute someone might snap their picture, say for a calendar, or for the cover of a fashion mag, that sort of thing.

Ralph looks around. A few shift from one posture to another. No one who is staring at someone wants to be stared at. There must be standard poses for the beautiful.

They are waiting, waiting.

The creature rings the bell again. Ding!

"What can I do for you?" the creature asks again.

The people here do nothing. Absolutely nothing. It is the

middle of the morning, that time of day when, were he not on a mission for his wife, Ralph would be at the Doggery, dipping, frying, but this crowd—all so able, all content—idle about and wait. For what? They don't carry books, so they don't read. They wait, and lounge, and glance at others in the lounge, evaluate the clothes others wear, and look at Ralph, evaluate, then look back at others, sizing up competition for whatever the game is they are all playing. What is winning here? Ralph wonders. What are the rules?

"What are all these people doing here?" Ralph asks.

"Making money," it says. "Of course. Or losing it."

"Lounging around?"

"Waiting for the daily results of the market. Some days it's up. Some days it's down. Most of the day, though, is spent waiting."

The creature rings the bell again, ding! and gives Ralph a look.

"What can I do for you?"

"I'm sorry," Ralphs says. "What?"

Then everyone looks at Ralph, everyone in the lobby, escorted in as he has been by this thing, which must be some important thing, and who asks what it is he wants, getting attention from this thing, attention which others here yearn to get, ready to check in—if this is checking in. Poor Ralph feels he is an object of their interest. Surely they aren't interested in his clothes. Is this disdain? There is something in all their looks: 'What might this new one do for us?' they ask. 'Or to us? Is he after what we're after, too, wanting what we all want, and will there be enough when he is done getting what he gets for us to get our share? Will we have to share? Is he a threat? Why doesn't he also have to wait? We are better than he is. Look at his clothes. Look at his hands. We were here first.'

All that they say in silent stares at Ralph.

Ralph smiles awkwardly. They do not smile back. Here smiles are signs of weakness. Now Ralph knows that. He frowns, then looks away.

"Are we going to see the Money Master?" Ralph asks the thing behind the desk.

The lobby falls completely silent. One hears nothing, not even breathing—if these others here are living; if they breathe. No one moves. Not even the creature who has brought him here.

"Did I say something wrong …?" Ralph says. "I didn't mean …"

"We'll see, we'll see, if you've brought a valid ticket. If your ticket's valid, I see it here. A lucky man. A lucky man," the creature says. "You've been selected. You've been reserved. You can go in. That is, to say, you go on from here. You're lucky. Very lucky. Tickets are rare. They're very rare. Few make it in. I don't know why. Some do. Some don't. You did. To get a machine, you must go in. You must learn to work it, then get to work, then buy it, then take it home, that is to say, get it out of here, we need the space, or pay us rent. We all want our own machines. All want to grow rich. Or grow even richer. Who doesn't? So many here, they wait and wait, and some go home, poor and ignorant, not all that different than how they came in. And some fail tests. And they stay here, most of them, and serve the rest of us. Make others rich until they die. Until I die. The horror of it. But, from time to time, some lucky soul is a lucky soul, and is selected, learns, and wins, and that could be you. That could be you. I see you are prepaid. That's very nice."

Ralph is polite. Philosophy has taught him patience at not knowing what someone means even when someone says something that should mean something, you would think. But he cannot resist a question.

"Why me?" Ralph asks.

That question bothers him.

"No reason. None at all," it says. "Everything is fate. Or luck. Or destiny. No one deserves what's here inside more than any other does. No. But sometimes you get lucky, sometimes some random fool—are you that fool?—comes in, and wins, and that gives hope to all the fools who are not lucky yet, who are not yet in, who are waiting, waiting. Hope does pacify the masses, don't you know? I'm telling you, without that, and belief in God, there'd be a revolution."

Ralph looks around and sees the crowd staring.

"Is that a book?" the creature asks.

Ralph indeed always has a book with him, never wanting to find himself without something to prod his thinking. It is, of course, his latest one, *Plato: On the Good*, and Ralph holds his place where he was last reading with his finger.

"Philosophy?" the creature says.

"Yes."

"You must be a socialist."

"This is Plato," Ralph says. "I don't see where Plato covers socialism. He just feels people should just get along and help one another." Ralph pauses. "It's a book about the Good.

There's nothing wrong with that."

"That's socialism, for sure," the creature says. He grabs the book and fluffs through the pages, as if fluffing pages transfers words and thoughts to mind. "You can't bring that in here. Plato is nothing but this Socrates in disguise. Socrates says this; Socrates says that. But that's just Plato saying what he wants. Which means he hides. Which means he's lying. Which means there is something that he fears. We should arrest him. Is this Plato coming, too? You can't bring subversive books in here."

"You've read Plato?"

"I've heard enough about him to know his books are dangerous. The minds in here are fragile. Don't pollute us with ideas. We've got our own ideas in here. We have our Good. You'll see. You'll see. You are here to learn, to do, and then get rich. No thinking here. Now I'd sign this register if I were you and get along. Get along."

The creature holds a pen for Ralph to use.

"Who are you?" Ralph asks again.

"If you don't know, then you don't know. But you should know, you know—you're prepaid after all—and thus you will know me, at last, I'm sure of it. I am the Sycophant. The Senior Junior Master here; which is to say, Assistant to the Master First Class, yes, and you're not, and no one else will be, at least until I matriculate and have my own machine and get rich while you are only you, and always will be. Which will be the one big difference between you and me. I am the Master's confidant, his second in command, Great Guardian of the Dollartorium, Guide to Sycophants in training. Which is you, if you get lucky once again. If your original luck holds out. If you pay enough. Again, I don't know. I don't know everything. If you think I do, you're wrong. But go on, go on. If you sign this book. If I let you in. If you pass the test. If your check is good and you pay the fees."

"The ticket …"

The Sycophant takes his ticket.

"The fees …"

"What fees? The ticket is prepaid."

"The ticket lets you in so you can pay the fees. None of this is free, you understand. This is the Dollartorium. Not some public school for anyone. This is a school for the elite, I say, at prices the elite can well afford. Five hundred dollars a day. That covers facilities, the pool, a place to park your car, and eight sessions of your choice. End of story. No more questions. Pay up. Sign this. Sit down. Don't talk. And let me take the next person in the line."

"Five hundred dollars is a lot of corn dogs," Ralph says.

The Sycophant gives him a look.

"We don't take corn dogs. We take Master Card and Visa, cash or check, or gold. And we're thinking we might add Bitcoins if you have a bit or two."

"I'll write a check," Ralph says.

Ralph is understanding even less now of the business of this business, or the process of getting rich—at least in these discussions. He is resigned, though. And determined. Ralph simply wants to do what he must do, learn what he must learn, get the machine that he must be getting, and get home in time for supper.

"I'll pay for just one day, then," Ralph says.

He writes a check.

"A check," the Sycophant says. He smells it, tastes it with his long narrow tongue. It shakes its head. "If you must. But there'll be a $50 check processing fee."

"Fifty dollars?"

"Cash is better, Ralph. Something solid. Most of our customers are broke. Gold is best of all, if you have gold, which I suppose you don't. Or banker's checks, but there's a fee for banker's checks. Who trusts a bank these days with all the thieves out there."

"Out where?" Ralph asks, looking around the room. Everyone drops their head and stops staring, and they all have been staring. "I have credit cards."

"That will do. But there's a fee for processing that and fifty to change the payment type."

As the Sycophant fills out the form, he pulls out a credit card processing machine.

"Whoa," Ralph says. "I'll get cash. I saw an ATM outside."

He didn't see an ATM, but it may be time he left. If he can get outside, he thinks, he can take a runner.

"Oh, Ralph," the Sycophant says. "You are rather fickle. I'll make the change—again—in mode of payment, but that incurs another cost. Two change of payment fees, and now a credit card cancellation fee, and some liability insurance in case something happens on your way to your ATM. A tornado, say. High water. Or a meteor strikes the earth. You cannot expect the Dollartorium to bear such risks alone."

"Just take this, then, and cash it," Ralph says.

He writes the check, including all the fines and fees before he gets tangled up in more charges.

"And let's get on with my sessions."

The Sycophant plucks the check from Ralph's fingers with a smile.

"There, there," it says. "That'll do, that'll do. And because you paid me promptly, I'll waive the background check. Which would incur another fee."

The Sycophant rings the bell and before the ink is dry it disappears.

THE MASTER

"The Master is excited you have come," the Sycophant says, returning to the front desk. "He'll be here to escort you back. The sessions begin soon."

Ralph finds himself sitting in the crowd near the front desk, and there he waits. The Sycophant returns to his desk to process other applications for admittance. "No," he says to one. "No," to another. "No." "Sorry, full." "I don't see where you are anybody I should bother with." "No." "No." "I could put you on a waitlist, but you'd have to wait ..." And so it goes for some time, the line moving forward but seemingly without end.

Despite all this processing, the crowd hardly seems to diminish. Some are dressed as businessmen with suits, ties, shiny shoes; and others—younger ones—in business casual; women, of course, blonde, buxom, seemingly fresh off some conservative talk show; a few quite hostile applicants, armed with various weapons giving unpublishable threats to 'let me in or else,' but the Sycophant is unflappable; and the usual coterie of citizens in a wide array of clown outfits, or MAGA hats, carrying resumes of their entitlements. There just seems to be no end to the number of people who want to get filthy rich.

And Ralph waits.

"Is he coming?" Ralph asks the Sycophant, who is busy working at the desk. Ralph sits alone on his own French-style gold-lamed couch, but he feels conspicuous in his common togs—the flour on his shoes, the grease stains on his apron. He grows increasingly uncomfortable in this crowd. Not to mention the hostile stares he gets from all those waiting in line or the sneers he gets from those declined admission.

The phone rings.

"He's coming," the Sycophant finally whispers to Ralph, and then he returns to the line in front of the desk to process further applicants. "No." "Void." "Failure." "You're fired!" "Not desperate enough." "Go away, I've said it before, I'll say it again."

"Maybe I should get my money back and go home," Ralph says.

"No refunds," the Sycophant says. "He's supposed to come." "He's coming." He's late." "He's busy." "He loves you." "He's teaching." "Give him a chance." "What if we gave everyone their money back?"

Ralph reads through worn and tattered magazines in the waiting area, coupons missing, pages torn, and puzzles finished. Most of them are financial magazines—*Money*, *Barron's*, *Forbes*, the *Journal*, all with news that is sadly out of date. Old financial promises—rising markets, falling markets, invest in this, sell that—opportunities lost, disasters averted. But Ralph looks through them—he would look through anything—to pass the time and avoid the stares. One should be doing something. Ralph would read a little more Plato, but he is afraid to reveal his Plato in this crowd.

"I wish he would come," Ralph says.

"He'll come."

Ralph walks around the large circular room. Mirrors line the alcoves. Bored, Ralph stares into the mirrors, sees himself, looks again, sees himself again, and wonders if he should go home. He likes his work at the Doggery. He feels it is part of something important, and making and selling corn dogs is important to him.

"What am I doing here?" he asks. "Maybe I don't belong."

"No, you don't," the Sycophant says. "But here you are."

The room is oval with marble floors, red wool rugs thrown here and there, and …

Suddenly, the Sycophant yells. "Watch out. Bow down! Duck!"

"You can't scare me," Ralph says. He picks up a magazine to read.

"Duck! Get down."

"I don't bow down to anyone," Ralph says. "No one here is any better than …"

The Sycophant falls to the floor.

"I may be one poor, stupid slob of the working class to you, my dear Syc, but this is America, and …"

"You fool!"

From the edge of the dome a hot air balloon enters the vast Dollartorium. A basket that hangs from it swings down and smacks Ralph on his head, knocking him to the floor. The basket circles around, trailed by guide ropes that hang to the floor. Some men—or things—from the audience grasp the ropes and slowly pull the basket down, then anchor it to a table. The Money Master rides inside. He attempts to guide this contraption, pushing buttons, pulling levers, and letting out hot air, but men on the ground guide the balloon down with the ropes and tie it off. Then, like everyone else in the room, except Ralph and the Sycophant, they drop their pants and bow to touch their noses to the floor.

"Master," Ralph says. He stays where he has fallen, flat on his back, head turned up.

"Forgive the faulty guidance," the Master says. "Today's market has been turbulent."

"I hope the market's closed now," Ralph says, raising his head slightly and rubbing the bump there.

"All hail the Money Master," the Sycophant says. The Sycophant pushes a chair against the table and helps the Master disembark.

"A most remarkable machine, don't you think?" the Master says to Ralph. "A deluxe basket. Fit for a billionaire. Buttons and handles for hiring, firing, selling, owning, profiting, chiseling, cheating, lying, hedging, fudging, tax evasion, the avoidance of all responsibility, and one that automatically suggests gifts for your congressman."

The Money Master pats the basket as he alights.

"Anybody who is anybody should have their own basket," the Money Master says.

"I've come for my money machine," Ralph says. "I'd like to get back home before dark."

"If you were an advanced student," the Master says, "I'd take you for a flight. The view is great up there. But you are required to take training sessions before you can fly this baby."

"Now?" Ralph asks.

"Ah. Master. Your Highness. Your Richness," the Sycophant says, interrupting. It now touches its own nose so close to the floor it can't be seen talking. Neither it nor the others have yet to stand up. "I'm so glad you're here. We're glad you're here. You look like a million. You look like a billion. Yes. And you have the best basket in the world. Better than anyone else's basket. Better. Higher. Longer. Lighter. More beautiful …"

Ralph stands and brushes the dust off his apron. He and the Money Master are the only two standing. The Money Master surveys his kingdom from his landing pad.

Ralph admires the flying balloon and its fine basket and controls. "Yes, this is something," Ralph says.

"That old thing," the Master says. "But it is good to swing in the ether. Up there one can see the pure movement of wealth. One can see how wealth flows through the world like rain falling on the rich. It trickles down from our heavenly assets to yours. It also smells better up there."

"If it's going to trickle, I should wear a slicker." Ralph is looking at the sky, avoiding as best he can seeing the sea of rear ends raised by all those who admire the Master.

"It gets me above the stench," the Money Master says. "It's a good place to work."

"You work up there?" Ralph asks.

"Oh, Ralph, my little corn dog maker," the Master says, putting his hand on Ralph's red cheek. "Let's not call what I do 'work.' Work is too much like …, well, work," he says. "I create wealth. I fabricate miracles up there, unconnected from the smelly real world down here, away from facts, from feelings, from little things, from stinky things, from ugly things, from people who smell, and grab, and touch. One can only embrace their adulation for so long. We wealthy ones prefer to live in baskets that dangle from the sky. In the sky burbs, as we say. And, if not in the sky, then maybe in a house just a little higher on the mountainside than the common riffraff can afford. Or maybe closer to the beach where the tide will wash away the flotsam of their dreary lives. Or on a few floors above the stinky city, away from the ratty humans on the streets. The more open space between the likes of them and the likes of oneself, the better I like life. Life without people, wealth without effort. All so good."

Suddenly the Master has a blank look on his face, and he closes his eyes. "In fact, I feel a current excess of wealth coming on."

He bends slightly at the waist and a look washes over him, a mixture of pleasure and pain as he tries to fart. But he fails.

"Ah," the Master says, standing erect, relaxing, and his eyes open as he stares at Ralph. "A false alarm," the Master says. "Just a certain inconclusive movement in the marketplace. But we're spared another stinking day on Wall Street."

At that the Master bends at the waist again, leaning forward, and lets loose a fart.

Ralph is startled. The Master climbs back in his basket. Eager to serve the Master, the Sycophant unties the hot air balloon as a terrible odor spread across the room.

"Another good investment has been born," the Master says. "Now it's time to begin your sessions. And you have been chosen from among the ranks of the poor to be an example to all of how a lowly wage earner can rise to the level of the one percent."

"I love your basket," Ralph says, not knowing how else to respond to the Master.

"In due time, Ralph," the Master says, "you may merit a basket of your own to float above the world and watch your wealth fall to earth and give birth to corporations."

"It does smell down here," Ralph says.

The Master turns nobs that light the flames that make hot air.

"For now, practice letting thoughts of money roll in your gut, churn up the ideas of business, deals, trades, contracts, legal suits, threats, promises, breech of promises, digest the creams and gravies of investments, relish risks and its rewards, sip the sweet wine of dividends, masticated on the cornbread of returns, gnaw on the weenie of your corporation, and then …"

A broad smile as the Master pats his tummy and lets loose both the ropes that have held his basket down and the gas of his thinking from within. The fart is loud.

"… then will the wealth you have created, the machine of your management, surge through your biggest asset, and emerge from the cornucopia of your abundance."

"I think I'm standing a little too close," Ralph says. "That gas can catch fire."

The Master smiles again, bends forward, and his face reddens again. But nothing happens.

"False alarm," he says. "An investment that has not yet matured."

"Please don't return until the market settles," Ralph says.

With that the Master floats away. Finally, the acolytes that have been bowing to the floor rise up and tearfully wave goodbye, dreams of riches dancing in their minds, promises twinkling in their eyes of hopes they will someday have their own basket, and hopes that they can watch Ralph's sessions and learn what is to be learned from the one who has mastered the art of being rich.

"It stinks in here," Ralph says.

"I know," the Sycophant says. "I love it so."

Part 3

THE SESSIONS

So finally, Ralph finds himself at the Dollartorium. Of course, we cannot expect him to simply buy a machine and take a few lessons in how to make money. Nothing is that easy, or who wouldn't do it? There is learning involved at the Universitatum Dollartorium—a series of sessions for wannabe wealthies. Deep changes in a person's psyche are involved. And, skills obtained for the art of bluster, and showmanship, entitlement, lies, or who would pay the enormous fees to attend? Plus, you get a hat that you can wear almost anywhere.

At U. Dollartorium there is only one instructor—the Money Master himself, the founder, the sole professor, the owner. Who else would we believe could teach the making of the deal and the wealth that will ensue except the Master? As is true in most modern higher education the curriculum here is focused on the rich, for the rich, about the rich, about feeling rich, looking rich, talking rich, marrying rich, while knowing nothing, yet seeming to know everything, the power of generating falsehoods, and about using the power of riches for those who have earned it, however they accomplished it.

A fleet of sycophants do the work of the Dollartorium—recruiting, submitting, processing, grading, filing, copying, arranging rooms, assigning seats, answering the phone, answering the door, paying rent, processing student loans, creating syllabi, and managing the all-important sports schedule.

By now these minor sycophants have processed Ralph's paperwork and payments, helped him choose his sessions, guided him to his classrooms, provided him with his seating chart, sold him tickets to curricular and extracurricular events, and otherwise filled his time in the process of getting him properly enrolled and on his way to becoming a supportive and proud alum. 'Don't forget us in your will when you die.'

At U. Dollartorium there is only one student at a time, and Ralph is it this semester. The hundreds of others who would take this course will be observers like fans at a college sporting event, to razz, drink beer, and tailgate. Much is expected of Ralph. Few are chosen. Few could do it.

Look! The Money Master descends again in his balloon, this time in the auditorium where the sessions are held. The audience stands, and a thousand admiring butts are raised to him among the wild applause, etc.

SESSION 1: WEALTH

Ralph has been admitted to the Dollartorium. Of course, everyone who applies is considered for admission as long as they are obsessed with getting rich and can pay the fees. Mrs. Ralph encouraged Ralph to attend. She had been deeply concerned about their status, about what their neighbors think since the Ralphs don't own a swimming pool or give a conspicuous amount to their church. She finds it embarrassing to be stuck in the middle-class.

Yet even Ralph is surprised on his first day of class to be picked to share the stage with the Money Master. Yet, then again, he finds he is the sole student in a mob of wannabes for this semester.

"I hope this won't be difficult," Ralph says as he steps to the stage.

The Money Master is dressed in an overcoat embroidered with red, white, and blue spangles and green dollar bills. His top hat glitters with gold, the very same outfit we've seen him wearing numerous times on television.

"Difficult?" the Money Master asks, his voice laced with sarcasm. "It will be the easiest thing you've ever done, Ralph. Who doesn't enjoy learning how to make money, then showing others how much you've made?"

The lights go down, two spotlights come up, one on Ralph and the other on the Master.

Ralph, of course, is firmly in the middle-class. Remember, he earns little running his corn dog shop in a small Kansas town where he makes the finest corn dogs in the Midwest. He has never been on a stage before, and here he finds himself hobnobbing with the likes of the Master.

The large, dark auditorium is filled with spectators—students, prospective students, alums, sycophants, fans, voters, the media, sponsors, friends. ... Well, okay, the Money Master doesn't have any friends. Friends are pests, after all, who only want something from richer friends, so you're advised to never make friends with the poor. No. Get rid of them.

Many in the crowd hold posters, blow horns, and wave flags. A man on the stage holds up various signs, 'Clap,' 'Wave Wildly,' 'Blow Your Horns,' 'Cheer,' 'Bend down and toot,' to which the audience appropriately responds. This is more than some boring lecture on money. This is an event.

"We need a desk, two chairs, a telephone," the Master says. He snaps his fingers, and two younger sycophants quickly push out a desk, a telephone, and two chairs.

"Amazing," Ralph says, noting the ease with which the rich get what they want.

The Money Master focuses on Ralph who shrinks down in his chair. Ralph still wears his petite little baker's hat, an apron spotted with flour and carries the green book he has with him, one of Plato's many dialogues.

"A little philosopher, I see," the Money Master says. He

looks to the audience. They respond with laughter.

"I always carry a Platonic dialogue," Ralph says. "Plato has the answer to so many problems." Ralph holds up *Plato: On the Good*.

"*Plato: On the Good*," the Master says, reading the title with a flourish. He grabs the book and shows it around the audience. They respond with more titters and a few toots. "Plato certainly knows about money," the Money Master says. He is laughing.

Ralph is taken aback. "I've never read that in any dialogue," Ralph says. He opens his book and searches for some reference. "Where did you find it?"

"Money," the Money Master says, "is pure Idea, and isn't that Plato in his purest form? Wealth is nothing but imagination, an Idea." The Master pauses. "Nothing is more real."

The Master waves Ralph's little book around the audience again.

"Say, someone has a banana," the Money Master continues. "What is that?"

The Money Master waits; the audience holds its breath. Someone tosses a banana on the stage. A few take out their pencils and pads, ready to take notes.

"That banana costs a dollar," he says. "So we say it is a dollar. The banana becomes an Idea, a dollar, so in the perfect world a banana is not a banana at all, but what it's worth, no longer a thing in the produce department with the other fruits, but a value." The Master pauses. "Everything has a value. And isn't that nice? A convenient dollar, a coin, a promise on a piece of paper, a bit, a byte, or merely a group of electrons constantly recycled in the eternity of computers to which someone has assigned a certain value. That is the perfect world."

The Master pauses.

"Plato would understand this perfectly," the Master says. He tosses the dollar back to whomever in the audience had tossed him the banana. The banana he keeps.

The Master takes a subtle bow and receives an ovation.

"We price a thing, it becomes that price—in Kansas City, Omaha, or San Francisco. That is to say, 'It's a dollar.' You don't need to plant it, grow it, water it, pick it, or pack it on a banana boat, because the banana is a dollar everywhere. You can put it in your pocket, save it until tomorrow, give it to some poor beggar to make him write you a poem."

"I'm hungry," Ralph says. "I like bananas. I'd like to exchange that banana for a dollar."

"Indeed." The Master pulls the banana from his pocket. "That'll be a dollar fifty."

"I thought it was a dollar," Ralph says.

"It was, but I've changed my price. Another beauty of Ideas. They can change on a whim. That's Plato."

More 'oooohs' and 'aaaahs' from the audience.

Ralph stares into the darkened auditorium. These spectators have obviously read the Master's own book, some perhaps having studied at the Dollartorium before. Ralph sees admiration in their gazes, hears love in their groans of delight. Ralph knows bananas, but the Master knows Ideas. Ralph reaches in his pocket for his lunch money.

"I'm hungry enough to buy it, even though …"

"It's two dollars now," the Master says, and he skillfully plucks two bills from Ralph's hand. "You're lucky to buy now. The price will go up soon. It's an age of inflation."

The crowd is chanting: "Money, money."

With his arms spread wide, his eyes closed, the Master flies around the stage like a bird, waving the two bills in his wings. The audience tosses coins on the stage in approval. Pennies, nickels, and quarters flash across the floodlights and tinkle to the stage.

"Money, money, money, money ..." The crowd grows frenzied.

The Master suddenly stops, raises his hands, and the crowd hushes.

"Yes, money, Ralph," the Money Master says to him. "A thing of beauty in all its glorious forms and possibilities— cash, rates, interest, puts and calls, things in the future for so much now and things now for so much in the future, risk and discounts, insurance, assurance, annuities. Unpaid taxes, monthly rents, weekly rents, rents by the hour, so much a minute, taxes deferred, the lack of taxes, guarantees, and letters of deposit. Depletions, derivatives, and royalties. Stocks, bonds, promissory notes, cash, checks and tenders."

The crowd has grown hysterical as the Master's list of possibilities grows longer.

Suddenly the Master turns to Ralph. "You. Ralph! Quick! Bring me a plate of interest compounded annually at 6%!"

"What?" Ralph has remained in his chair, but now he pulls up his legs and wraps his arms around them. This knowledge of all the forms of wealth flows at him too quickly. He has been carried away by its endless forms. "I don't think you can … A plate of interest?”

“Of course, you can’t,” the Master says, breaking in. “Wealth is not a thing you can serve on a plate.” He is speaking to the audience. “It’s invisible, eternal, lovely. It’s an Idea. A promise. A deal. A bet. A hedge. Here, quick,” the Master continues, holding out his hand as if there is something for Ralph to give him. “I’ll take a double helping of options, thank you.”

“Options?” Ralph says. “I don’t think …”

“Of course, you don’t. Options are invisible. They are Ideas. Up or down, puts or calls, today, tomorrow. Who needs the actual banana?”

Ralph’s knowledge of corn dogs doesn’t seem to be helping him understand money.

“Wealth is invisible, vaporous, fragile, pure, which exists only as long as others dream and believe.”

“Believe who?”

Silence throughout the auditorium.

“Me!” the Master finally says. His eyes are closed, his face turned upward to the vaulted ceiling of the auditorium. At that the adoring crowd quiets. “And now we end our session,” the Master says, eyes closed, as the tinkling of coins thrown on the stage diminishes.

Ralph looks up to where the Master looks, but all he sees is the ceiling. Is he learning what he has come to learn, he asks himself, or is he beginning to be dazzled by the mindless wonder of it all?

SESSION 2: THE IDEA

They take a break. The Money Master circles the stage, his hands clasped behind his back. He wipes his forehead with his sleeve. As the next session is about to start Ralph sits at the desk, his Plato unopened. A bell rings. Ding!

"What do you sell, Ralph?" the Money Master quickly asks. The Money Master turns, puts his fists on the desk, and thrusts his face into Ralph's.

"I sell corn dogs," Ralph says modestly.

"Corn dogs," the Money Master says. He snarls like an unfed dog. He shakes his head. "Corn dogs are so forgettable. Sell something that sells, Ralph. Something everyone wants. For which they'll pay cash."

He bends forward, leans over Ralph's back, looks with some intensity over Ralph's shoulder. Ralph dares not look up. There is no help for him. He is on his own. He is the only student in the Dollartorium, and the crowd looks on.

"People come for miles to buy my corn dogs," Ralph says. "I make them fresh every morning. 'You see them dipped, you know they're fresh,' so we like to say."

"That's it?" the Money Master asks. "That's all?"

"Isn't that enough?"

"Ralph, Ralph, Ralph."

The Money Master clasps his hands behind his back and circles the desk in a profound walk, looking down as he shakes his head, mumbling 'hmmm's', and 'haw's' and a 'my word' or two. Then he stops, looks up, looks down, looks up, frowns, looks down again, then up again, then smiles.

"Let me rephrase," the Money Master says.

He wraps his arm around Ralph's neck and pulls him close.

"A corn dog," the Master says.

He seeks inspiration from the vast dome above. There are no stars in this vault, but the light glistens off something that must be silver. Not stars.

"A corn dog is a corn dog. But what is a corn dog really?" the Master asks.

"A corn dog …" Ralph responds.

"… is?" The Money Master gets nose-to-nose with Ralph.

"… is a hot dog," Ralph begins. He is tentative.

"A hot dog? A hot dog?"

The Money Master shakes his head.

"A hot dog is so nothing. What do your customers want? What is in their hearts?"

"… dipped in batter?" Ralph says, but hesitates. He looks at the Money Master, not so much to answer that question as to avoid it. He clarifies. "… in corn meal batter?"

"Nope, nope, nope," the Money Master says.

He lets go of Ralph's neck.

"Nope. Nope. You'll never get rich selling 'corn meal.'"

"… fried in grease …"

"Nope. Not fried in grease."

The Money Master shakes his head and holds his chin as he stares at the ceiling vault.

"Grease is a turnoff. No one eats grease anymore."

"… served on a stick."

There is a pause. The crowd in the auditorium is silent.

The Money Master ponders the question to himself. He circles the desk as he mutters words that might be a better answer.

"Grease. Stick. Dogs. Corn …"

He expresses strings of things, of words, phrases, images, possibilities. His palms are open—not to Ralph, but to the gods—if such exist—perhaps the gods of marketing, or perhaps the god of corn dogs … no, surely there is no god of corn dogs—his arms are out, as if he juggles words, seeking a pattern.

"You are thinking of 'things,' Ralph," the Money Master says. "You'll never get wealthy selling 'things,' especially 'things' made with cornmeal, grease, and pig."

"But I already do make a nice living …"

"Wealth, Ralph. We seek wealth. You must sell more than things. People already have things, all the things they need, all the things they want, not things they had yesterday, or things they are unwilling to make space for. Your people are hungry, Ralph. Anxious. Full of fear. Sell them pleasure. Comfort. Love. Safety. Give them a hero to follow. A god to worship. Not a corn dog."

"What do I sell?" Ralph asks.

"Pork bellies."

The Money Master is lying on the desk, staring up at the scoreboard that hangs from the dome. We're halfway through the first half of this round. He has his hands clasped behind his head, and his legs bent at the knee, his feet dangling over the edge of the desk. The Money Master is comfortable and relaxed, unlike Ralph, who sits in a chair at the desk, hands folded and in his lap.

For a moment Ralph says nothing.

"Pork bellies?" Ralph echoes.

Almost a question, but one doesn't question the Master.

"You must sell something, Ralph, something that's something, something you count, something you price, something that's pure value. Yet something that isn't something, either. Pork bellies will do nicely. What is a pork belly? Many a fortune's been made selling them."

"I see," Ralph says.

But he doesn't see, of course.

"Have you ever seen a pork belly, Ralph?"

The Master sits up.

"Only when a pig turns over in the mud. I've seen hams, and hocks, and fresh pork shoulders."

"Pork bellies are not pork bellies," the Master says. "Pork bellies are promises."

"I see," Ralph says.

But he doesn't see.

"Nobody buys bacon. Nobody buys hogs. You got your big hogs. You got your small ones. You got your fat ones. You got your sick ones. You got your boars. You got your sows.

You buy a pig, but who knows what you're getting. So, you buy a pork belly, instead, and you get something that doesn't grow old, or grow mold, or need refrigeration. You get a pork belly. Which is to say, you purchase the idea of pork."

"Of course, you do," Ralph says. But he's not at all certain that you do such a thing at all, because he doesn't quite know what it is to buy something that doesn't exist.

"And in the world of business, we don't buy bacon, or jowls, or hams, or shoulders. We don't hold it, store it, shave it, or smoke it. We don't even eat the damned things. There is nothing to eat. No. I say, we buy pork bellies."

"Oh," Ralph says. "Pork bellies." Almost as if he knows what he is saying.

The Master turns a bit on the desk, his head on his elbows as he stares at Ralph. We almost hear the audience, the fans, the enthusiasts, writing all this down.

"You buy pork bellies, and you sell them."

"First, I'd wash off the mud …," Ralph says.

The Master sits up and bends forward.

"But we only buy what we sell, and only sell what we buy, all at the same time," the Master says. "So, a pork belly is bought, and then it is sold, so there is no need to have something in between. No need at all. There are no pork bellies. What you have is a deal, and that is business."

"Of course," Ralph says.

He must figure this out later.

"There's nothing to have. They don't exist …," the Master says.

"No, they don't."

"… except as ideas. As promises."

"Ideas," Ralph repeats as if to signify he understands.

"It's just a promise. An idea."

"Yes. An idea. Like Plato."

There. Now he thinks he understands, not because he understands, but because he has a reference that means he should. Still, he doesn't.

"I'm sure everyone sees that," Ralph says.

He holds up his book, the Plato he's never without.

"Pork bellies," the Master says.

"Yes. Pure Plato."

"Ideas are what's real," the Master says.

"You've read Plato?" Ralph asks, as if now he might be understanding this lesson from the Master.

"So, to get rich you create an idea. Then you shape it. Morph it into something that others can see, that others can want. Then make them want it. You turn your idea into their desire. Then their desires give rise to their appetites. A yearning for pleasure. A quenching of hunger. An end to their pain. Love for the lonely." The Master slaps the table. "And everybody gets an orgasm. And you give them this in the shape of a corn dog. Do it well and you can charge an extra fifty cents for everyone." The Money Master thumbs through Plato. "It's all here, if you read between the lines."

"I'll have to take another look at that dialogue…"

"Whet their appetites, Ralph, sharpen their desires. The wealthy get wealthy when they whet, and sharpen; and heighten, and fret, hone, and bone … Wealth comes from stimulations, elevations, all solved with cash for cash. And isn't that the modern economy? Ralph, the secret of wealth comes in knowing how to end the craving, heal the itch, alleviate the lust, assuage the fear, whether the suckers know it or not. Sell it for all you can get. And do it again. And again. You'll see how wealth accumulates."

"So, you're saying I don't sell corn dogs."

"No, Ralph. What you sell is sex. The corn dog is just the package."

SESSION 3: ON TERMINATION

There are two chairs on the stage, one for Ralph and one for the Money Master. The stage is like a boxing ring, with ropes around a square and seats beyond for the audience, where the sycophants sit who have come to see and study the secrets of vast wealth.

Spotlights glare down on both the Master and poor Ralph whose shadows stretch across the canvas. Ralph breathes heavily. It has already been a long day of thinking and learning the ways of the rich, and Ralph, being the Master's only student, has been the focus of all his intensity.

The bell rings. Ding!

"Now, show me, Ralph, how it's done, how to get rid of dead wood in your business," the Master says. "Streamline. Kick up the profits. You're in charge."

"Dead wood?" Ralph says. "I'm in charge?"

A sellout crowd fills the auditorium. Many are eating popcorn, or corn dogs, and drinking beer. Others are smoking, and a layer of that smoke cuts above the crowd.

Ralph slumps back against a corner post.

"Certainly."

Certainly? All Ralph knows for certain is he knows very

little—about money, and business, and what it takes to flourish in the modern economy. If anything is true, he thinks, it is that nothing is true. And what he has always assumed he has wrongly assumed. And that corn dogs are a silly way to make a living. And that Ralph is not in charge of anything. And that the Master is the Master. Still, Ralph is on stage, the crowd anxiously awaits his reply, and the sooner he starts, the sooner this will be over.

"You are the boss," the Master says. "Sit at your desk."

The desk sits in the middle of the ring. There is an old rolling desk chair at the front of the desk, and across from it is a larger black leather one.

"I sit?"

"Sit!" the Money Master says, then he smiles and relaxes.

"Okay." Ralph sits in the wobbly wooden chair.

"You're playing the role of the boss," the Master says.

"But you're the boss," Ralph says.

"Yes, I am the boss," the Master says. "And you must do what I say which is you're the boss. You have brought me into your office to fire me. You will fire me because you can. Because you are in charge. Because you are you. Because you sit in the big black leather chair … Get up, Ralph," the Master says. "Get out of that little chair. Sit in the big chair. The good chair. The leather chair. I work for you. Make your employees sit in little chairs. Old ones. Wobbly ones. Bosses have big butts. Big chairs, big desks, little walnut in-and-out trays, big plaques with their names in big letters, their big diplomas on the wall. Size matters here, Ralph. Class matters. Walnut matters. You're posh. You're expensive. You're in charge because I've said you are."

"Okay …"

"It has come to your attention, Ralph—not all that much ever does—that my salary is an expense to you. It lessens your wealth. If you fire me, you can add my salary to your own. So, it's time to cut the fat. That's me. Anyway, things have been going along nicely. You've got a surplus of corn dogs. Enough hogs have been slaughtered, and enough pork has been ground to make a six month supply of wieners. The casings stuffed. The corn shucked. The cornmeal ground and bagged. So, it's time to run up profits. Cut expenses. Raise your prices. Limit your overhead. Sell off the inventory. Drain the assets. Sell some stock. Sell lots of stock while profits look good. If you need help, you can hire a temp, or an intern. Your numbers will suddenly look good. And if you need some help, there are plenty of people who need jobs and temps who work especially cheap. No benefits. Oh, how I love the sound of that. And interns will work for nothing at all. So, fire me."

"Okay, Mr. Master." Ralph sits in the large leather chair. "If you insist."

"You've invited me into your office … 'Thank you for staying late,' you say. Or 'Thank you for coming in.' Or, 'Good afternoon. I hope things are going well with the family.' Or, 'How about them Celtics?'"

"The Celtics are terrible this year, Mr. Master," Ralph says.

"You wanted to see me," the Master says. His tone is humble, meek. "You've made me stay after work. You've made me come into your office. I've missed my bus. Now, take control of the situation. Fire me."

"Thank you for coming in today. I'm sorry to say your

work has not been going too well, and I'm sorry you've missed your bus, but we're going to have to let you go …"

"You can't fire someone sitting down."

"You told me to sit."

"Don't do what I say. Do what you must. It's you or me, Ralph. Fire me before I realize how unfair all this is—hell, I do all the work, I've shared all my ideas. Say, firing me will hurt you deeply. I'll be left unemployed and broke, but it's the numbers matter, don't they?"

"I'm sorry …"

"… but do you care? Fire me!"

"We're just pretending …"

"Fire me!!!"

"Okay. Thank you for coming in Mr. Master. Your work has not been going too well, and we're going to have to let you go …"

"You're still sitting. Don't give me time to think. I might pull out a gun and shoot you. And if I did, you'd deserve it, you capitalist piece of crap."

"I'm not …"

"Take command, Ralph. Crush my spirit. Stand up while you make me sit. Be the boss."

"Thank you for coming in today, Mr. Master. Due to factors beyond our control, and the needs of my exorbitant management salary, and the numbers, and maybe the fact that your work has not been going too well, we're going to have to … Please sit."

"Don't explain anything, Ralph. Act. All your employees are idiots, they steal from you, they loaf around, they want your job, they want your money, they will try and take control unless you … Your losses are their fault. Tell me to sit. Sit! Sit! Make me sit. Shout, 'Sit!' Damn it! Then slap the table. Hard! Like this."

The Master slaps the table hard. He nearly stands, then he sits, and the audience sighs. An incident averted. This is not a polite event. No one applauds. They are afraid.

"Okay. Okay. Thank you, Mr. Master for coming in today. Sit!" Pause. The Master sits. "Your work has not been going too well …"

"No. Get rid of me. Do it quick. Think, if I had died in my sleep, which is what you'd prefer, you wouldn't have to go to all this trouble. Never apologize."

"I see …" Ralph takes a deep breath. "Sit! It would have been a better day today if you had died. So you've brought this on yourself. Now I must fire you."

"Better, but …" The Master regroups. "Have you ever been fired, Ralph?"

"Uh, well … yeah." Ralph is embarrassed. He mutters. He stutters.

"Draw on that, Ralph. That pain. Picture the asshole who fired you. How unfair you think he was. How unfair he was! How he shamed you in front of your friends, your family. Draw on that. Dump your anger on me. Blame me for everything that's gone wrong in your life. Hate is the great motivator. You're the boss. I've been the source of all your problems for far too long."

"But when I got fired, the guy was actually right to fire me …"

"He was an asshole, Ralph. You are never wrong. You are

an entrepreneur. Whatever he did to you, he should have known better. He hurt you. He lied. He was unfair. He had no right. He didn't listen. He stole your ideas. He stole your woman. He screwed your dog. Get angry, Ralph, and get even."

"No one has …"

"Just imagine it, Ralph. It doesn't have to be true. This is a teaching moment! It only sinks in if you believe. Jesus wants you to fire me."

"Okay," Ralph says. He shrugs his shoulders, clears his thoughts.

"Firing me, remember, will make you a man," the Master says as he shrugs his shoulders and prepares himself to take it. "It will make you a bigger man. Better than me. A man women will respect. A man women will want."

Slowly Ralph feels himself becoming more the boss, infallible, the source of all thought, of all truth, of all meaning, of all action, of all good things now and forever more. He swells up with pride. He is free to do with as he pleases. Yes. He relaxes his shoulders. He is in control. Yes, he is in charge. He has nothing to worry about. He sits back from his desk, leans back in the leather chair, taps a pencil on the desktop. He is busy, busy, busy. This employee is a bother. Ralph doesn't want to fire him, but he must. It is his duty. He is a threat. The audience expects it. "Thank you for staying after work. I know it is Friday …"

"Perfect choice of time, Ralph. You're on a roll."

"… because we need to talk."

"Yes," the Master says. "Imagine yourself turning a knife in my heart. Enjoy it."

"We need to talk about your job. Your work has not been going too well …"

"Pour it on, Ralph. The momentum builds. This guy has made you look like a fool. He wastes your money. He makes you look weak. Unmanly. A threat to your happiness. You'd rather be with a woman, dining, drinking, screwing. You'd rather be walking your dog. You'd rather be drinking a martini and talking to the olive. But he draws you down, he keeps you here. He is incompetent, a threat, and he must be fired. Tell him, Ralph."

"It is better for you if …"

"It's all his fault. Say that."

"You have brought this on yourself."

"Yes, Ralph, it is Friday afternoon. The office is quiet. Everyone else has gone home."

"Sit, please," Ralph says. He points to the small wobbly chair. He looks into the Master's eyes. "Sit!!" Ralph says it firmly, then slaps the desk hard.

"Yes, yes, relish the moment."

Ralph stands, goes to the window, and looks out over the city. It is growing dark. It is early winter. Cars come and go on the street below, occasionally honking, streetlights, headlights.

"I look away," Ralph says. "Over the cold gray streets above the lonely city. It has started to snow."

The Master sits at the edge of his chair, his hands clasped.

"This is harder for me," Ralph says, "than it is for you."

"Nice," the Master says softly. What greater reward is there than seeing your student succeed in his lesson?

Ralph pivots to face the Master whose chair wobbles.

"I've given you every chance."

"Do I see a tear, Ralph?"

"I look at you. Then I slap the desk again."

Ralph slaps the desk, and the Master is startled.

"You are finished here," Ralph says. "You are history. Terminated. Fired. You no longer work for us. We no longer want you. You must leave the herd. You've made me stay late. I am missing my supper. My dog needs to shit. My children are hungry. You must leave and leave now."

Silence.

"Lovely, Ralph."

Ralph reaches under his desk and brings out a cardboard box.

"Oh, yes." The Money Master says. "The box."

"I push the box across the desk," Ralph says.

Ralph breathes hard and fast, his face turns red as he holds onto the desk, staring at the Master.

"Say it, Ralph!" the Master says.

"Put your things in the box," Ralph says. "Leave your ID card and the office keys on your desk. We will mail you your check because I don't want to see you. Ever. Ever. Again."

Long pause. Ralph has come to believe in himself, he's the boss, in his office in some busy city. It has grown dark. It is twilight outside. The only light inside shines on the desk. He hears the muffled sound of traffic, cars and busses, a car horn from time to time.

The Master slowly smiles, takes the box and turns to exit.

"Excellent, Ralph," he says as he hesitates. "You have the heart of an ideal boss. You make your Master proud."

SESSION 4. THE BUSINESS PLAN

"I'm a banker, Ralph," the Money Master says. "What's your plan for all your corn dogs?"

The audience has been seated to await the fourth inning. The hawkers go through the audience, stopping at every row to sell peanuts, beer, and—special today—corn dogs, because Ralph, a maker of corn dogs, has come to the Dollartorium to learn the secrets of getting rich. His wife wants Ralph to learn to get rich so they can become one of the one percent.

The Money Master is on the stage. He is the very image of a banker. He smokes a banker's cigar. He wears a jacket— red, white, and blue—over his pants and shirt, also red, white, and blue, spangles covered with dollar bills; his top hat in red, white, and blue. His gold-tipped cane is at his side. His tie certainly was once a flag, ripped up and resewn to become a tie so long it hangs over his crotch. He sits at the desk—in a black leather chair, of course. He pounds the desk.

"You have come to me for money," the Money Master says. "You need a loan from the bank. Now what's your plan?"

Ralph still wears his apron and cook's hat, a blue workman's shirt and shoes covered with cornmeal from where he makes corn dogs. Just yesterday he was still doing real work in his Corny Doo Doggery. Now he has come to the

Dollartorium to learn the secrets of acquiring wealth and ascending into the elite so he will never have to do real work again.

"Do I need a loan, honored sir?" Ralph asks, hardly knowing how to properly address a banker, much less a loan officer in a posh office where everything, even the in and out trays are made of walnut and other fine woods. Humble seems appropriate in the face of such wealth. "The Doggery is getting along fine. I pay my bills and use my own money to finance what I need. I live a rather modest life …"

"You need a loan, Ralph," the Money Master says, interrupting, "We never use our own money for business. Business is business. Your money is your money. You're here to get other people's money to use as your own. That's the way things are."

"I beg your pardon, sir, but I'm not sure anyone wants to loan money to a corn dog maker …"

"You beg my pardon!?" the Money Master says. He leans forward over his desk. "Never beg, Ralph. Heaven's sake, I'm a banker. People give bankers money for free, and in return bankers loan out that money at exorbitant rates." The Master laughs. "And if that isn't a good business deal for bankers, then I don't know what …" But the Master catches himself before he reveals too many secrets. "In the meantime, if we bankers need even more money, we get it from the government for a small fee to keep America great . If there's a better scam, I'd like to hear about … That's why you always see bankers at your charity balls."

"I'm here for a loan," Ralph says, eager to get on with the lesson.

The Money Master relights his cigar, puffs and looks powerful, as is so necessary to his station as head of a bank.

"You need a plan for why you need money," the Master says. "Give me a plan, a very good plan, and I'll loan you money. But I need to know I'll get my money back, and soon, and more money back than I've loaned you." Puff, puff on his cigar. "So, here you are, Ralph, begging for money …"

"You said … not begging …"

"Give me your plan for your Doggery."

"I've only been at the Dollartorium a few hours. I'm not sure I have a plan …"

"You need a plan," the Money Master says, interrupting Ralph. He picks up the book Ralph has been carrying, *Plato on the Good,* and thumbs through the pages. But he quickly dismisses it. He leans down and hugs Ralph. Then he takes Ralph's hands and stands him up. "A plan, Ralph. You must have a plan. So you can wheel and deal. That's the way it's done. A wheel. A deal. A plan. A name. A buck. Some luck. A plan. A plan! A marketing plan! You have to have a plan, Ralph, or how you will get from one place to another, from poor to rich, from no one to somebody?"

The Money Master holds both of Ralph's hands as they whirl about on the stage in front of the hundreds who have come to watch a lesson being given at the Dollartorium. Dollar bills fly off the Money Master's clothes.

"How do you sell what you sell for how much? That sort of thing," the Money Master says.

"I only run a corn dog stand," Ralph says. "I sell corn dogs, and I sell them at a fair price. We try our best to serve our friends and neighbors the best corn dogs possible, too."

Whirl, whirl. "I guess that's my plan." Whirl. Whirl. Ralph is breathless. The Money Master says nothing, so Ralph feels he must continue. "We make them fresh, and we serve them hot. You can see them dipped if you come early. People buy them and they seem happy. Then they'll come back, some twice a week. I make an honest living there, and I hope I can do it until I die."

They stop dancing. The Money Master stares at Ralph.

"A corn dog stand?" The Master stares at Ralph. "A good corn dog? A fair price? That's not a plan, Ralph. That's work. One will never get rich merely working for a living."

Ralph looks around. The audience is waiting. He needs a bigger plan. Everyone knows that.

"We do grow our own corn," Ralph continues, seeking to give the Master a better, more acceptable plan. "We raise our own pigs. We slaughter them for meat, then we grind them up and stuff them into wieners."

"Work, work, work. You're making me sick, Ralph," the Money Master says. He has stopped dancing, and he has returned to his desk and to puffing on his fat cigar.

"We make very good corn dogs," Ralph says. "We have our following."

Clearly Ralph has little idea of what constitutes the modern business plan. He has ideas, enthusiasm, perhaps even a good idea and the desire to make it work. But he needs a business plan. Things must change.

"So, you have a product, a corn dog. A place to sell your corn dogs. But no plan." The Master shakes his head, clearly disappointed.

"I don't know," Ralph says, struggling to find the right

answer. "Maybe …" Ralph sits down across the desk, wiggles in his seat, draws on the desk with his finger. "Maybe …" Long pause.

"What, Ralph? What's your plan?" The Money Master makes it sound like the answer is so obvious.

"Maybe it would be nice to open another stand on the other side of the river."

"Another stand?" the Master says, incredulous. "That's your plan?"

"Another stand. I've often thought about that. Maybe my daughter could run it. Or, I have this cousin …"

"Another stand," the Master says. He shakes his head. "I suppose it could be a start."

"On the other side of the river," Ralph says, hoping this is the sort of plan a banker might want to hear.

There is a pause in the conversation, and a scattered coughing from the audience who await the Master's response.

"That's it?" the Money Master says. He sighs. He rolls his eyes. Puff, puff. Ralph pouts a bit. Ralph has in fact sometimes thought about opening another Corny Doo Doggery, but there are many obstacles to that. He has always concluded, too, that he is satisfied with what he has, with doing what he does, so why put that in jeopardy? And who would run another stand? And where would he get the money to build it? And what would happen if … Questions, questions. Yet he does not want to disappoint the Money Master who has been so solicitous about the business Ralph holds so very dear.

"Well," Ralph says. "Maybe …"

"Maybe, maybe, maybe, maybe," The Money Master shakes his head and puts out his cigar with vigor. "What,

Ralph? Maybe what?"

"Well, I have thought—this is really my wife's suggestion—but maybe …" He looks up. He sucks in his lips, and looks down, because he has never talked about this idea to anyone before, other than his wife. "Maybe, I've thought, you know, not like I have to, but I've also sometimes wondered if, well, we could add onion rings to the menu," he says. Now he breathes deep. Changes like this can change so much else at the Doggery. Can he grow enough onions. Can he grow the right kind? Can he dip them and cook them to keep them fresh and hot like his dogs when they're sold? He speaks these last few words quickly, and under his breath, and without looking up.

"You open another stand, Ralph? And you add onion rings to the menu?" the Master says. "That's it?"

There is another period of silence as the Master waits for Ralph to come up with something else, something that is to the Master's way of thinking a real plan.

"There is this building across the river we could rent," Ralph says. He has considered this, too. He's had his eye on a place that might make a nice little corn dog store. It could even have a drive through, whereas now customers must come into the Doggery to get their corn dogs. "There are some people who are reluctant to drive across the river to get a corn dog, you see. And some of them don't want to get out of the car. And … well, everyone likes onion rings, I think. And we got the fryers, and we use the best grease. So onion rings make sense. 'You see them dipped, you know they're fresh,' just like we say for the corn dogs. You could then …"

"Ralph, Ralph, Ralph." The Master just waves Ralph off, shuts him up with a gesture of his hands. "I don't know what to say. Your thinking is so small." And here, intentional or not, the Master glances at poor Ralph's crotch. With the thumb and forefinger of his right hand, he gives an estimate of length.

The Money Master stands. His clothes shed dollar bills. He thinks better on his feet, and it is time for him to do some thinking, some showing and not just telling. The Master strides about, pacing back and forth, back and forth, hands clasped behind his back. He turns to Ralph. "Okay," he says with a firmness that precludes any argument. "Pretend I'm you, and you're me."

"But I'm not you. And you're not …"

"Pretend, Ralph. Imagine. Dream a little. This is a plan that will set you up for the rest of your life."

"Okay," Ralph says.

"Now, you ask me for my plan." The Master wiggles his fingers, urging Ralph on. "I'm you. You're me. Ask away."

Ralph pauses. "But if you're me, you don't have a plan."

The Money Master frowns. He tolerates no sarcasm. Business stuff is serious stuff. Ralph taps his fingers on the table. "I'm the new you, Ralph. You are a banker, rich beyond words, floating through life on other people's dough."

"So, I am you—who is someone else—and you are me—but not *me* me," Ralph says, "No, a new me, and you—who is me—are here to ask me—who is you—who is a banker … something."

"For a plan," the Money Master says. "You ask me for my plan so I can borrow your money."

"What's your plan?" Ralph asks. This is no time to question what he is being told to do. This is the time to do and obey.

"Plan?" the Money Master says. "Plan?! A business plan? My business plan?! You're asking me for my business plan?"

But the Master is not confounded, no, not like Ralph, for he is not Ralph. That is, he is not the old Ralph. He will be the new Ralph. Ralph reborn. A better Ralph. A business Ralph. A Ralph on his way to wealth and happiness. The Money Master, playing Ralph, rises, clasps his hands behind his back and paces back and forth. He looks up, he looks down, he reaches the edge of the room, stops, turns and paces back the other way.

"Yes," Ralph says, getting into the spirit. There is something about playing banker that he likes. He, too, stands and follows the Master around the stage, Ralph's hands clasped behind his back, as well, his head up, head down, quick turn, follow, turn, follow. "Yes, what's your plan? *What's your plan?*" he demands of the Master.

"I'll give you a plan!" the Money Master says, stopping suddenly, turning suddenly to face Ralph. The Money Master shakes his head, then looks up as he gives shape to an idea, but—"No, no." He stops and begins his pacing again, back and forth, back and forth, Ralph following him in lockstep.

"I have it!" the Money master says loudly, stopping, and turning again. "Yes. I have it!" He is looking up at the ceiling, at the heavens, and then he slams his hand on the desk.

"Yes?" Ralph says meekly, quietly, unprompted.

"Right here," the Money Master says. "Yes, right here!" He slaps his hand down on the desk again. "We start right here. Right smack dab in the middle of nowhere, this is where it begins. One little Corny Doo Doggery. What a story. Right here, in the heart of things. It begins here. And it begins now," the Master says.

There is some light froth on the corners of the Master's mouth, and from the look in his eyes he sees something the rest of us don't see, something beyond anything at all. The future. Ideas. Platonic forms. Money. The Plan.

"Nobody's watching us here in this little store in this little town," the Master says. "Yes. We work in secret. The competition is asleep. Good. So, we borrow money from a bank. Good. Some little bank that doesn't know any better than to loan money to a corn dog stand. Good." The Master pauses, then whispers, "Corn dogs."

Suddenly he slams the desk again with the palm of his hand.

"Yes," the Master continues. "In the middle of nowhere! Yes, that's what I say. Perfect. Corn fields. Pig farms. Yes," then he stops and turns again suddenly, "And smiling pig faces. That's our logo. I see it now. The home of the smiling pig."

Ralph stands motionless, his jaw sagging a bit, his eyes wide. The Money Master waits a bit, then resumes his pacing. When he looks Ralph in the eye, Ralph nods as if he gets the picture, even if he doesn't, not yet, but he nods some slight agreement.

"Good," the Money Master continues. "Clean. Good. Small. Oh, those are all good. 'A family business.' Yes. 'The Smiling Pig.' 'The Organic Pig.' Perfect. What's not organic about a pig? Or dirt. Or sunshine, corn, and grease so clean you can swim in it. Yes."

The Money Master spreads his hands to the sky, as if he

sees what no one else can see. Ralph looks but doesn't see it all just yet.

"Then," the Money Master says as if the words are there for him to read, as if the vision is a film he's watching, "We smash every other restaurant in town."

Oh, there is love in the Master's eyes when he says that. Passion.

"Corn dogs, the one true food. The only food. The healthy food. They're good for you. A corn dog a day and you'll live forever."

He pauses to look at Ralph.

"We start with one more frigging corn dog stand on the other side of town, right? Then, another, and another in other little towns around. Not picking on the big guys. No. But one by one, Mom, then Pop, we kill them off. 'Who wants chicken fried steak when you can have a Corny Doo Dog?' Competition, that's America. Then we gobble the rest of them up. Dwight. White City. Emporia. Yes, we move up to Emporia. And where they were, we are now. We spread rumors of ptomaine. We steal their employees. We grow our little chain of corn dog stores. Corny Doo Doggeries here. Corny Doo Doggeries there. We buy out, shut up, run over, burn down any bastard that gets in our way, too. And then, when we got a lock on this state, we move on. And on … Into Nebraska. Into Oklahoma." Then, in an almost dreamy tone, "Texas." The Money Master grows dreamier and dreamier, not because his energy flags, but because his words have moved he himself, from reason into a state of ecstasy. He becomes more passionate. Water wells up in his eyes. "And … we raise our prices."

In a brief moment of lucidity, he looks at Ralph and smiles. Ralph doesn't move, except to look closely at the Money Master, to follow his eyes, to follow his gestures, and Ralph swallows, almost as if he senses the danger in all this excitement.

"Yes. We raise our prices on everything. Because now, oh, god, what are they going to do? You have made corn dogs part of the American dream, 'enough corn dogs and you might live forever,' this becomes the American dream. Oh, god forgive me, I love this. And next …"

He looks at Ralph and pauses. Ralph licks his lips, unsure of what is being asked.

"Next?" the Money Master asks again.

Ralph shakes his head, he doesn't know what, but he is not afraid. He is eager for more. He wants to hear the rest of the plan. He wants it to be a plan of his own.

"… television! Of course!" the Money Master says, with a kind of certainty that states the obviousness. "We all love television. And if it's on television, it is a part of us. We cannot live without it. The loneliness. The silence. So we advertise and place our product in the hearts of all our viewers, every movie star we love eats a corn dog as we watch them in our dark living rooms, and we, too, yearn to have a corn dog, just like them. Then, 'Get a Corny Doo Dog, the only true dogs.' 'One of them Ralph's Corny Doos!!'"

Ralph listens carefully to the Money Master's words, his vision. He sits gently, looks up, and waits.

"We get publicity, Ralph. We reset reality. I see books about corn dogs. Movies about corn dogs. A corn dog reality show. A documentary that 'We are what we eat,' and, 'We want to be a Corny Doo Dog."

But then there is a pause. The Money Master relaxes a bit and holds his chin, rubs it, and rubs it.

"But what's the concept?" the Master asks. He is not asking Ralph. Ralph knows nothing. Ralph does not have the vision.

"Yes, the concept," Ralph repeats, without any real notion of what he is saying, but he so much wants to be a part of this lesson. Marketing will transfigure his modest corn dogs, after all.

There is a long pause. Then a false start. "A bun … No." The Money Master rejects his first thought without discussion. Long pause. "Salt … No.' 'Grease … No.'" Long pause. More chin rubbing. Then as if some warm fire inside spreads throughout his system, the Money Master leans back, rests, is all smiles, all confidence.

"I've got it," he says. "Fun. That's what we have on a stick." In this word, he has bundled up his vision of the new world of the Corn Dog. "Corny Doo Dogs are fun."

The Master waits. Ralph says nothing. The conversation continues inside the Money Master's head.

"No," the Master finally says to himself. "That's not sexy enough."

Then the glow returns to the Master's cheeks. His eyes mist up.

"Oh, I know. I know," the Master says. "If you want a big dick, buy a Corny Doo."

The Master claps his hands.

"Yes. Yes. That's it. Big dick! If you want a big dick, buy

a corn dog. Now who doesn't want a big dick. That's a concept that will sell corn dogs."

But his enthusiasm stops cold.

"But that leaves the women out, doesn't it?" the Master says. "And they buy corn dogs, too."

The Master does not expect Ralph to answer. The Money Master is creating.

"Women don't want big dicks …" Lots of thinking. "But … they want men with big dicks … So …"

Light. Warmth. Enthusiasm.

"What we're selling is: Fun for men with big dicks and the women who love them."

Each word a gesture; each sentence a vision.

"Perfect."

There is a broad, soft mewling and mild applause from the audience. Another winner has been created at the Dollartorium. Even Ralph finds that kind of thing in this sort of world somewhat reasonable. Even exciting. A certain warmness settles in between his thighs.

"It's American. Yes," the Money Master says. "Pure American. Red, white, and blue, get out the flags, and fun, and big dicks. We'll buy some ads for the Super Bowl and during the Sweet Sixteen. There will be fun and flags, and ads with girls where you can almost see their tits. And you're watching TV, and you think, oh, man, if she bends just a little more, you'll see her tits, and you watch, and you laugh, and that's fun, and flags, and red, white, and blue. And this is fun for guys with big dicks. And it's American!"

The Money Master stands, his hands framing his

thoughts against the sky. He slaps Ralph on the back. He's on a roll. This is beyond corn dogs. This is marketing.

"We grow the chain of Doggeries. El Paso. LA. Providence, Rhode Island. Tucson. We make a plan with legs, Ralph. We break out of our region and into the world. Nothing can stop us. You folks in Denver—corn dogs. 'You want one or two?' Of course, they want more than one. Once they're hooked on the six-ounce dog, you shrink it to five ounces, save a pig! Which leaves them longing for more. Yes, men with big dicks and the women who love them."

The Money Master is satisfied. He shakes his head to congratulate himself on such wonderful thoughts.

"We get our product into chain stores," he continues. "Distribution, that's the ticket. Walmart. Target. Kohl's. If they sell candy, they ought to sell corndogs. Stock them near the register, a display with flags, and, boy, is it fun, and a poster of the girl on television, right there by the register and you can almost see her tits, and because you want a big dick, you buy two, and flags, and fun. And you know you're American!"

Ralph stands at attention. This feels like war. He feels like a soldier. He's ready to go over the top. To victory!

"Then, Ralph, we'll take the show to Kansas City, right? Then Dallas, Baton Rouge—yes, down there to all god-fearing, Bible-loving towns full of white folks cause, if you got the white folks, you got America, men in trucks, and boys on skateboards, and suddenly we're in business, buddy, and it's time for Broadway, for the musical, dancing corn dogs, music, fun, and flags swaying, and if they sway a certain way you might see a little tit ..."

The Money Master pauses to rifle through the desk for a pad and pencil to write this all down.

"It's a plan," the Master says. "But we need a name for what we're selling." The Master stares into space as he chews on his pencil. He ignores Ralph. After all, what does Ralph know about the mysteries of marketing?

"Corny Doo Dogs," the Master says. "No, no ring to it." He shakes his head. "We need a name that travels, that endures, that will become part of the language. Like Xerox. Or Coke. Or Kleenex. No," he says. "We need sex. Like …" Then, after a pause. "Schlong! How's that? I like it." Another pause. Another shake of the head, more denial. "No, no, it has to sound American, so maybe Pud. Puds! Pud's Dogs. Pud's House of Dogs. I mean," he continues, "Two Puds, 'cause one's not enough."

He writes that down and then he chews on the pencil again.

"Yes," the Master says. "Get it in the air, into the language, everywhere. Make it American."

The Money Master tears off the paper, folds up the sheet and puts it in his pocket.

"Good work, Ralph," he says. "We got the concept. Where do you take it?"

"I'm not sure," Ralph says. "Am I still you?"

"Well, if I'm still you, and I am," the Money Master says, "then you must still be me. Everyone has to be somewhere. What do you do with this plan?"

"I don't know." Ralph swallows. "I'm excited, though," Ralph says. "I mean, flags, and Walmart. And that little breast thing. We are going to need more corn dogs. Maybe I should go back home and start dipping."

"Think big, Ralph," he says. "Think bigger. Think business. A corporation. A corn dog cartel. Then what do you do?"

The Master closes his eyes and waits for Ralph's answer.

"Well," Ralph says. "I guess we expand. Set up manufacturing. Distribute, supply chains. Keep them fresh, of course. Invest in our infrastructure …"

Ralph is eager to please the Master now.

"Oh, Ralph!" the Money Master says, disappointed. "There is no end to the drudgery you seem willing to do. But work is for workers. You provide the concept, you shape the idea, they do the work. But then, what does the entrepreneur do?"

Ralph hesitates. His eyes are down. He looks at his desk. He bites his lower lip. He feels like he is failing. How is it he knows nothing of this process, of what real businesspeople do? No wonder he is not rich.

"Add fish tacos to the menu?" Ralph quietly suggests.

"No fish tacos, Ralph."

The Money Master pulls up a chair and faces Ralph. The Master's voice is low. He makes what he is about to say seem confidential.

"Sell," he says.

Ralph looks up. He is surprised.

"Sell what? I haven't done anything yet."

"Time to sell the whole thing," the Master says. "You have a plan. It's time to get your money. Sell it all quick before someone finds out you have no idea what you're doing."

SESSION 5: BANKRUPTCY

Ralph looks worried. The crowd has returned from a brief intermission to take a leak and fill up on refreshments—that is, more beer, and ideally a second corn dog. They have taken their seats and the lights have dimmed.

Ralph sits on the small stool in one corner of the ring. He looks tired. Heaven knows what he is thinking. But he has learned a lot today about the nature of capitalism and the skills needed to succeed therein. During the intermission the Money Master has been busy, talking on his cell phone, buying and selling, or hiring and firing, or scheduling or rescheduling this event or that.

Ding!

The Master closes his phone. Ralph stands and brushes off his apron, adjusts his baker's hat, and slowly approaches the front of the desk where the Master is sitting. Let the learning resume.

"So, Ralph, it is time for any questions you might have," the Money Master says. "You look a little worried."

"I am. What if things go wrong with my new business?" Ralph says. "What if I make a mistake? What if I find myself overextended? What if I go broke?"

"Things can never go so wrong you can't make a profit.

Nothing is so dire you can't scam a few bucks off the top."

"But all this planning, and borrowing, and change," Ralph says. "It's new to me. So many details, any of which could go …"

"What's the worst thing that can happen, Ralph?" the Master asks. "You close a factory? Who cares? You are forced to lay off a few people? You raise your prices? You must cut costs and buy cheaper ingredients? Rich people make mistakes all the time and people suffer so profits can still be made. Whose problem is that?"

"Say, if business is bad," Ralph says. "Really bad. What if I am wrong about what people want? Or how much people will pay for my corn dogs?"

"Now, there you go again, being negative."

The Master does not look at Ralph. He is looking over the audience that stretches out on all four sides of the ring, the bleachers rising high up to where the rafters meet the seats and the fans and students, alumni and contributors, are lost in smoke. The Master is smiling. He has seen this sort of behavior before. He knows negative thinking can kill the entrepreneurial spirit. Think positive, he thinks, or don't think at all.

"Say, no one wants my corn dogs anymore," Ralph continues. "No one comes in to my shop. No one comes by to watch me dip corn dogs in grease. My corn dogs grow cold. My money runs out. I have to close the Doggery. Forever."

Again, the Master speaks, not to Ralph, but to the audience. For the Money Master, this event is not only a matter of teaching Ralph this and that. He has a message to give to the world, about him, what he does, how he does it, how good he does it, how much money he makes, and his happiness they should envy. He wants everyone to know how he likes what he does. How much he likes how he does it. How much he makes in doing it.

He closes his eyes and raises his head as if the sun is shining full on his face. He likes to be loved. Don't we all? He smiles. He shakes his head. He is confident he knows the answer, that he knows best. He opens his eyes and looks at Ralph. All is quiet. All are listening.

"It never has to be that bad," the Master says.

"But I could lose all my money."

"You can't lose your own money, Ralph, if you don't risk your own money in the first place. Only a fool would put his own money where it could be lost. You use other people's money. Never risk your wealth. Oh, Ralph. Poor Ralph. Business is bad. So bad for poor Ralph."

The Master puts his hands on his heart, and groans, and stands, and twists about, then falls on the desktop, then twists around on the desktop, then groans, then falls to the floor and twists around on the floor, then holds his chest where his heart would be—if he had a heart—and …

"I'm sorry," Ralph says. He pulls out a handkerchief and offers it to the Master who seems to be in great agony.

The Money Master suddenly stops his pratfalls.

"Why are you sorry?" the Master asks. He stands, fully alert with no emotion on his face. He brushes off his coat. "Never be sorry, Ralph. Never apologize. Heavens, you're only going bankrupt. People go bankrupt all the time. Yes, yes, yes, their business might lose everything, that's true, but not if you keep a distance between yourself and your companies. Pay yourself well while things are happening. Salary. Perks are even better—less taxes. Golden parachutes so you make money even if you fail. Bankruptcy is a way to wealth as good as any other. If you are bankrupt, I say, 'Hooray! Hooray!'" The Money Master stands on his chair and does a dance. "I had a deal," he continues, "And I failed. Hooray! My creditors are after me. I can't pay my bills. Boo-hoo. Well, if I can't pay my creditors, who loses? They do. How can the company pay if there is nothing to pay them with? So, never shell out a cent of your own. And much of what you've borrowed, you should have taken out before in salary and bonuses."

"I'm so sorr …" Ralph starts, but he catches himself. He is not supposed to be sorry. Not here, anyway. "That's too bad," he says instead.

"Too bad!" the Master says. "Too bad!?" he shouts.

The Master looks quickly left to right, then right to left, then under the desk, then under his shoes.

"Who says it's too bad? Too bad. Too bad." He pauses. "Too good! Now that's the truth."

"Too bad you failed," Ralph says. "Back home, back at the Corny Doo Doggery I worry all the time about money coming in, money going out, about having enough to pay my bills. I worry if there is enough business, and about cash, and costs, and wages, and rent. Hog feed's gone up; did you know that? Gotta feed the hogs so we can have meat to grind into corn dogs. What if the hogs go hungry? What if the the corn dries up? The wife will be mad if business goes down. My daughter will be out of her job … I guess even rich people have problems."

The Money Master's face comes close to Ralph's, and he

waves his finger in the air, then pokes Ralph in the chest.

"So you lose your business, and your neighbors think your dick is too small," he says. "You're broke, despised, hated, ridiculed. Your friends have lost their investment. But you've paid yourself well, and you're rich. If you are a smart businessman, that is. So, there. And a little bankruptcy will not stop another fool from loaning you money again if you can sell them a new dream of infinite riches."

The Money Master leans back, folds his arms, and smiles.

"Borrow so much the bank can't let you fail, Ralph," the Money Master says. "They'll only lose if they sue you. The bigger the mess, the more money they'll give you the second time around. And having access to as much money as you want, isn't that the definition of being rich? Who cares where it comes from as long as you're wealthy and can spend what you have. You are the one who controls your wealth."

Ralph is taken aback by the truth in this. He puts his finger to his lips to think.

"But won't I look ridiculous, a failure who grows rich?" Ralph asks.

"Indeed, you will," the Master says. "But looking like a fool, isn't that the perfect cover for a thief?"

This time there is no applause from the audience. The truth is too profound.

"The power to fail profitably is the beginning of all greatness," the Master says.

SESSION 6: THE GREATEST SALESMAN

"The highest art a salesman can embrace is to sell money for money to people with money," the Master says. "Money is the fastest way to make money."

The Money Master circles the stage, his arms stretched high above his head, his hands clasped, victoriously shaking to the heavens, showing himself to the crowd on all four sides of the ring. He smiles. He is the victor, whoever his opponent might be. The entire middle class, one might suppose.

"I only sell corn dogs," Ralph says quietly.

Ralph pays attention as he sits at the desk, craning his neck as he follows the Master's movements. He is determined to learn all there is to be learned, in order to absorb these winning ways. Not that he wants to learn so much, but he is anxious to finish and go home.

"I shouldn't say 'salesman,'" the Master says. "It is the entrepreneur who must glean the skill of using money to make money from money."

"I see," Ralph says. But he doesn't see.

The Master stops his circling and again sticks his face close to Ralph's, so they stand face to face, nose to nose. Unless you have an excellent ringside seat, you cannot see much of this closeup action, but the cameras are rolling and they zoom in on the lesson to be seen on the screens overhead—the sweat, the spit, the Master's forceful lips moving as he makes his important points.

"If you want to sell money to someone, Ralph, who do you call?" the Master asks.

There is an uncomfortable pause. Ralph stares at the phone on the desk. Time passes. He clearly doesn't know who to call. And he knows nothing about selling money, or who does it, or who might want to spend money to buy any money he sells.

"I was hoping we would be done by six o'clock," Ralph says. "I'm supposed to be home for supper."

"Who is the best person to call if you want to sell money, Ralph? The answer is obvious."

"I don't ..."

"People who have money."

"But why would I sell money to people who already have money?" Ralph asks. "Why would anyone buy ..."

"Because with money everyone wants more."

The Master wins again. He clasps his hands above his head and shakes them as he circles the ring in a slow trot. There is applause. Crazy, noisy applause. From the crowd. Whistles. An air horn.

After a moment, the Master continues. "We all want more money, even if it costs us money to get it."

Another few laps around the stage. Less cheering now. The crowd wants more from the Master.

"But we're not talking money-money, Ralph. We don't sell money-money. Coin dealers sell money-money. And gold, and diamonds, that sort of thing."

That word 'thing' sounds dull in and among all the Master's talk of money.

"We sell the pure and holy idea of money. We sell endless possibilities that set sail on a sea of cash. People paying now for money they'll get later. Or paying later for money they get now. We sell cash—cash for things then or things for cash now. Cash or credit. Plus interest. We buy back—no returns—and we take checks, IOUs, and promissory notes. Cabbage, dough, and shekels. Piasters. Lira. Euros. Cabbage, bacon, pork. All sorts of paper and promises that are money. Mortgages, loans, and lines of credit. Confused?" the Money Master asks.

"A little," Ralph says.

"Afraid?"

"A little more than before."

"Excellent." The Money Master does his little jig, then he turns out to the crowd, although ostensibly talking to Ralph. "Fear is good for the economy. And good for those who buy and sell. Confusion, too, is a wonderful tool. Confused people buy more. Fearful people pay more for what they buy. The idea is to get them confused, afraid, and horny, then sell them something, anything, and tell them that that is what they want."

SESSION 7: FINANCE

Lights dim again after a short break. Silence prevails.

Ralph wears an apron and a paper hat, as he did when he first arrived—how long ago was that? The Master has given him a pair of pointy Italian shoes which Ralph has put on, and the Master ties a tie around Ralph's neck, then finally crowns him with a Derby which covers his paper hat.

"There, Ralph," the Master says. "Now you look the part of a businessman. You're management now. Who wouldn't hire you?"

"That's nice," Ralph says. He doesn't feel like he looks nice, nor does he feel like he's a part of anything, but this is school, and he is here to learn. "I want to be hired, I do," he continues in a semblance of enthusiasm. Ralph is slowly coming around to the Dollartorium way of thinking. It has begun to feel Platonic, as if that way of thinking is a perfect philosophy for business. "What are you hiring me to do?"

"You do nothing. A good manager gets others to do the things that need doing. So, you needn't bother to learn any actual skills, even if you have none already. Your job doesn't require them. Your only duty is to make sure everyone else is working hard and you are getting the compensation you are due," the Master says. "Nothing less."

"I like my hat," Ralph says, even though he doesn't like it. He doesn't know what else to say. He is trying to be polite.

Ralph has never worn a real hat. That is to say, he has never worn a hat that had no purpose but to sit on one's head and give the wearer a sense of authority. This hat fits well enough, he thinks. Not as snug as his baker's hat which he is wearing under his Derby, but by now he assumes he won't be baking anything, so anything else that sits on his head is fine with him.

There is chortling from the audience who have ascertained that Ralph is naïve. He has done nothing all his life but work. He has thought about his work, how to mix the materials to put in corn dogs, the way to dip corn dogs. But he has never thought beyond doing, nor has he considered what all that might mean in terms of something as abstract as compensation, how many dollars he should earn for every hour of labor, how much salary he should get for a week of dipping corn dogs. That is, he's never thought of work as just a form of cash.

He waits to learn as he fidgets on the stage, dressed, he feels, like a clown. He feels perfectly dressed to be useless. He has never worn a tie or shoes that are not only tight and uncomfortable, but so fragile they would be ruined if he wore them while he did any actual work. One drop of grease on those Italian shoes, and the shine is gone. Lean forward at work too far and his tie will dip in the grease. And if it rains, his hat will sink down on his head.

The Master clears his throat. "As a manager," he says, slightly adjusting Ralph's Derby, "you set your own compensation. How much you can get is how much you want, and that starts with how much you value yourself."

Ralph wonders what his compensation is at the Corny Doo Doggery. He doesn't think he has any.

"How much compensation do you make dipping corn dogs, Ralph?"

"I pay myself a small salary," Ralph says, a little cautious.

"No! No! No!" the Master shouts. He turns around, waving his arms. "Salary? Pay is a pitiful measure of the successful businessman. Let's not talk about salary. Let's talk about compensation."

There is silence. One could hear a nickel drop in the auditorium if anyone in the stands dared drop a nickel. No one does. Not even a penny.

"Here is what pay is," the Money Master says. He hugs Ralph. "We love you."

"Well, thank you …" Ralph blushes.

"Pay, like the hug, means nothing, of course," the Master says.

"I sort of enjoy …"

"Wages are nothing more than a token, a symbol, a hug a business gives to keep the riffraff working."

"I don't …"

"And pay is taxable, unlike compensation with which we endow the wealthy."

"Well, doesn't the law require that …"

"Compensation is the ticket. What do you want, Ralph? Can we pay you another hug? We love to give them."

"No." Ralph pauses. Again, he feels out of place. He may never get rich unless he can understand this better. "But don't we pay people who work? How else am I going to get rich?"

"Not that way," the Master says. He points to the heavens with one finger as he journeys in circles around Ralph and the desk, smiling. He knows what he knows, and Ralph doesn't. The Money Master waits until Ralph gives up waiting for a better answer. This is all so confusing.

"Maybe I should just stick with corn dogs and ..."

"The rich don't care about 'pay,'" the Master says with disdain. "If you insist on getting paid, if you want a salary, if you want us to take out deductions and pay taxes, okay, we'll pay you one American dollar a year."

There is a collective gasp from the audience. They are familiar with this game, but it is new to Ralph, these nuances, the twists, the beauty of the deal.

"One dollar?" Ralph says. He hesitates. "I make more than that in an hour at my Corny Doo, and I consider myself barely paid at all."

"Of course, Ralph. How wise you are not to take your compensation in salary. A dollar is not nearly enough to get rich. You'll never have a big house at that rate. Your new Tesla, your dream will always be a dream. And doesn't your wife want a swimming pool? How are you going to manage that? Does your Senator know your first name and sponsor bills to deregulate your corn dog business, or give you tax write-offs and government grants? No. 'Salary' is nothing in the world of business. Do you like paying taxes, social security, Medicare? All those are taxes that come out of a salary. Your salary, Ralph, which your own company pays!"

"I like Medicare," Ralph says quietly, but such heresies are all too easily booed in this crowd.

"We all like Medicare. But who wants to pay for it? Not

the rich. No, no, Ralph. You don't want to earn a salary."

He succumbs. "I guess I don't."

"I guess you don't," the Money Manager says. "You, Ralph, want a compensation package designed especially for your position as an entrepreneur. It's how the wealthy get wealthy. With few taxes, or no taxes, and benefits galore—so you can keep your compensation and write off your living expenses."

"I just sell corn dogs," Ralph says.

"A manager, an entrepreneur doesn't 'sell' corn dogs. Ralph. He manages the flow of things: the manufacturing and distribution of corn dogs, the incoming tide of cash. You must start at the beginning, the moment you're getting hired, to negotiate your package." The Money Manager pauses, clasps his hands behind his back, and paces around all four sides of the stage. Then he resumes in somewhat less of a frenzy. "First, never take what you are offered. Take more. They want you cheap, so they offer you less. Whatever they offer, say more." The Master winks. "And a fancy title is essential. A fancy title will earn you more than sweating in some common slot. A little negotiation, a bit of whining will get you a corner office with windows. With walnut in-and-out trays. Make the company pay for your new Italian shoes. They want you in costume; make them pay for the costume. Insist on transportation to and from the office when you go. A Tesla is nice. A limo is better. Let them send you to meetings at exotic resorts all over the world. Membership in a ritzy golf course. Dinners at obscenely expensive restaurants. A butler. A tailor. Escorts. Your own chef. An expense account for your executive life and all of your pleasures. Your sacrifice merits compensation, so you demand …" The Money Master pauses.

"$300,000 annually, all in bonus. And a hug."

"And a hug?" Ralph asks. "How big a hug?"

"You already got your hug."

"That's compensation?"

"Not enough?" the Master asks. "Okay. Okay. Then $400,000. And two big hugs."

"That's hardly …"

"Okay, okay, okay," the master sys. "Then $500,000, but not a penny more. And no more hugs. You're hired, Ralph. You certainly drive a hard bargain. Now, set up your expense account, get a haircut—no, a style—buy some new togs—all Italian and tailored, or silk and Hong Kong—and put a lock on your office. You won't be able to sleep or sober up after lunch if you can't lock your door. Hire your girlfriend to do nothing but guard your office. Show up at work from time to time but not on a schedule. And the first job at work is to schedule your lunch. At the office talk about your shoes, your boat, your golf handicap, make sure everyone beneath you works hard at whatever needs to be done, and be perfectly sure they know what they are doing because you certainly don't."

"$500,000 is a lot of corn dogs."

"It's no more than you deserve for keeping American business the envy of the world."

"How can anyone afford me?"

"They can't, Ralph! Isn't that the point? You are worthless, especially when you actually show up for work or start making decisions. As soon as possible you should fire everyone you can, as fast as you can. The fewer parasites with their salaries sucking off the corporate assets, the longer you stay on the gravy train."

"Fire everyone? Is that good?"

"That's great," the Master says. "Profits go up. Expenses go down. The stock goes through the ceiling. Great for the economy."

"But the workers …?"

"Trim the fat. When you hear that, you know you are talking to an entrepreneur. Worthless fat is trimmed and watch the prices of your stocks."

"I have stocks?"

"Indeed, you do. That's where the real money is. And your earnings are all in capital gains, tax free if you have the right accountant. The price of stock is the price of stock, and when the price of stock goes up, sell, so even if the business goes down the shit hole, you're rich. The numbers are what you care about, and it's all just numbers. Ideas," the Master says, tapping his head. "Plus a little show biz."

"That sounds wonderful, sir," Ralph says. "But I can't afford to buy stocks."

"Good news, Ralph. You don't have to buy stocks. Options must be part of your compensation. You're management. You negotiate. 100,000 shares a year for … $10 a share."

"Ten times … That's a million dollars, Mr. Master. I'll never be able to …"

The Money Master laughs. "Options, Ralph," he says. "A promise to sell stocks you don't buy until you sell. You buy at $10, then sell at $100, all on the same day. And you pocket the difference. "

"So $90 a share times 100,000 shares …"

"You're rich, Ralph, and who's the worse for it?"

"My god," Ralph says. "Is that legal?"

There is tittering in the audience.

"Plus," the Money Master says, "it's all capital gains. No payroll tax, no social security, and—with a little bit of planning and a shrewd accountant—no income tax. Just an occasional little contribution to keep the politicians happy so they can twiddle with the tax code here and there. It's perfectly legal. Or legal enough. It's what you can get away with. You want another hug?"

"No, please," Ralph says. "No more hugs. With a deal like this, I'd never quit."

"Don't quit," the Master says. "Exactly. You must wait to be fired."

"Fired?" Ralph hasn't considered that. Just when he begins to worry such a gravy train might end, he learns it must.

"Of course," the Master says. "You don't intend to actually work there, do you, Ralph? You merely start the thing, then sell it as quickly as you can. Open the doors, then close them before something actually happens inside. Just make sure you escape the coming disaster. No one wants to buy any corporation where you are the executive. You are an idiot. We all know that. Privileged, entitled, and you have no idea of how to run a business."

"Well, no," Ralph says. "But I thought that's what I'd be learning. All I really know is how to make corn dogs."

"And the best part, Ralph, is that you have negotiated a lovely severance package. So—medical coverage for the rest of your life, a yacht, an apartment in London free and clear, another five years' salary, and maybe another million shares at

$8 a share … No, get out of your business as fast as you can—and this should be obvious—before someone makes you responsible for the mess you've made. Once you're fired, you get your parachute, relax and kick back, and soon you get started on your next business venture."

"Again?"

"Again, and again. Failure after failure, it's too good to stop."

A smattering of applause. Someone from the mass of onlookers, Ralph's fellow novitiates, tosses a nickel on the stage. Then comes a quarter. In such a way the audience begins to show its pleasure. Another entrepreneur is born. More coins. More.

Slowly Ralph smiles. He is beginning to get it. He sees the beginning of the end.

SESSION 8: FLIGHT OF FANCY

The Master's empty balloon descends to the ring. The sessions are over. Ralph feels good. Now he feels he belongs. He feels he's learned something. A few days of reading Plato should help him organize his thoughts.

The Money Master steps into the basket that brought him to the auditorium earlier.

"Ralph," the Money Master says before he lights the burner so his balloon will rise with hot air. "Step in with me. We have one last stop. It is time you meet your own money machine."

Ralph eagerly climbs in. He bows to the audience and the balloon lifts up.

Ralph believes he now understands the secrets of success. He has learned what he has come to learn, and he will leave with a plan. When he returns to the Doggery, people will see the new him, what he's become, all he might be. Perhaps even Phyllis will be pleased.

Below him, the crowd applauds. He can feel their envy. Good. Because he is now prepared to hire, fire, sell, plan, think right, think quick, think wrong, make money, set price, charge more, bluster his way along, and smile without meaning it in the least.

The two of them float off in the Master's basket.

"Someday," the Master says, "you can afford your own basket."

"My own basket," Ralph says dreamily. Far below, as the two of them ascend, the audience has all gotten on their knees and bared their butts in honor of all those who rise to the level of the one percent, not because they love them, but because someday they hope to fly exactly like that in their own hot air balloon.

Ralph is all primed and eager to ascend to that percentile now.

"I can hardly wait to fleece the poor."

"We will not waste our time with the poor," the Master says. "The poor have no money."

"Then we should just cut the fat and kill them all and be done with all their troubles," Ralph says. He feels wise with his new education under his belt. He feels he understands his mentor and his ways.

"Ralph," the Master says. "There are limits. We need the poor to pay their taxes. Someone must, after all. Let the government fleece them. And they are good when a war comes along, to pay for it and to keep the rest of us from being bothered."

"Oh." Ralph realizes that being rich is a process of lifelong learning. There is so much he has yet to learn.

"Plus, the poor make the rich feel even richer than we are. If nothing else, we are at least not one of them. Anyway, the poor don't cost much. They work for little and get even less. Whatever they cost, we earn more from their labor, so—crazy as it is—they work to help us get our new boats and houses with bedrooms and baths we don't even need. And they love us for it. Often they worship us, too, for being rich and doing what rich people do. How many television shows are there about poor people, unless—from time to time—they are poor people who want to be rich? And don't we love the criminals? The poor especially like rich criminals. They admire our corruption. The poor want to be us and to do what we do. And they are content as long as they think they possibly might. The most the poor can hope for is to own their own homes. But, ha, we hold their mortgages. We manage their retirement plans. We manipulate the prices of their investments. And they have nothing to invest in but us and our companies. Oh, Ralph, they are our pets, our little toys. We would be bored without the poor to kick around, don't you think? And they without us, they'd most likely become both bored and a danger to the current social order."

"You'd think they'd be squealing."

"On the contrary, Ralph. As long as they want to be us; they'll not want us to change the slightest. They want us to tell them what is good, what is right. They insist we be rich and act like it. Look, the best colleges are colleges where the rich people go. We package the poor people's dreams and sell their own dreams back to them—votes, dignity, freedom, sex, fears—My god, Ralph, we even sell them water." The Master stops at that, turns to Ralph, for even to the jaded Master, this is a nearly incredulous accomplishment. "Water, Ralph!" he repeats. "Water falls free from the heavens. But we put it in little plastic bottles and sell it back to them … Water!"

"Water."

Ralph is on the verge of tears. This is soooo good. This man is soooo smart. He's gotten soooo rich. Where, Ralph thinks to himself, has he been all his life?

"Are people really all that stupid?" Ralph asks. The Master says nothing but navigates his hot air balloon smoothly across the horizon. No answer required.

Part 4

THE CITY OF MACHINES

The Master floats with Ralph in his hot air balloon into another grand auditorium, a vast workshop that extends behind the Dollartorium, acres and acres of dome-covered space filled with machines, wheels and gears that turn, pistons that thump, hammers that pound, steam—poof, poof—all in an effort to create wealth.

"What a vision," Ralph says.

"Yes," the Master agrees.

The Master is pleased with Ralph, his new student. They land on a small balcony, and from there Ralph admires the acres filled with the machines of the workshop. Another dome covers it, painted with figures of the Master in various poses, buying, thinking, selling, golfing, or just sitting at his desk, thumbing through magazines, looking at pictures of himself.

The area below is divided into miles of small squares. In each square, a machine sits on its own platform, and machinists sit on their machines and pull levers, push buttons, step on pedals. Smoke pours out of exhaust pipes, and steam puffs out of engine petcocks. All these machines are connected to each other by pipes, tubes, and wires. Ralph wonders what is being pumped in, and, whatever it is, where does it go?

"Wealth," the Master says. "Here it's manufactured in all

these new money machines, our latest creations. Aren't they lovely?"

Each machine is different except each has an identical box attached to the end of the machine.

"That looks like money coming out the end of some of those machines, dropping there into those boxes," Ralph says. He hears the clinking of coins and the crinkling of dollar bills which seem to come from all the little boxes at the butt end of these many machines. "Is that how it works?" Ralph asks. "Is that how cash is made?"

"So one must suppose," the Master says.

"Nice."

By now Ralph has become a devoted student of the Master, believing all his promises and all the Master tells him. He recalls the hubbub at lunch hour back at the Doggery, much like the chaos here, except this seems to be less work, each person alone on his or her own machine, and money the result rather than corn dogs sold to customers. He could do this, he thinks. Here he could easily read Plato while he runs such a machine, and he would grow rich so as to please his wife, and he would not be so tired and covered with corn meal at the end of the day. No corn to plant, no pigs to slop.

"It's time for you to learn how to run one of these babies," the Master says. "I think you are ready."

The Master leads the way downstairs and through back stairways, then out to the arena to the machines, as well as the mass of vendors crowding the pathways with their booths and tables, yelling out prices, bids, numbers, selling or swapping, investing or gambling, all making deals with each other.

"We call that selling stocks," the Master explains.

"Whose stocks are they selling?" Ralph asks. "And who sets the price?"

The Money Master gives Ralph a look as if he may have forgotten a lesson or two already. Ralph almost looks like he wants to make a bid, he is ready to buy or sell something to someone, to get into the game.

"They are buying and selling nothing," the Master says. "Only promises. Here we see they are making the perfect deals. The minute a vendor sells what he calls a Bitcoin which is a promise to buy it back later. In the meantime they come out to the midway and the seller does his best to tell everyone how smart the buyer has been, so by the time the buyer wants to sell his coins the price will have gone up, and that will net the buyer some wealth. Well, others hearing that ought to kick up the demand for more coins, and with that comes higher prices, more wealth all around. Nobody has done anything but make a few deals, and all have grown richer on nothing at all, on promises at best, on faith and dreams. No real work at all. Ralph, here we are making the pure deal."

Ralph's head begins to spin as he tries to understand how all this works without any work at all. It is a skill well beyond a man whose life is simply making and selling corn dogs. But he has learned now why he's never gotten rich.

"Wealth moves here in such pleasant harmony," Ralph says. "Ideas of things are so much neater than things themselves. Shadows are preferred over objects. Plato would approve."

Ralph follows the Master as he leads him through this world of gray, well-oiled machines, the sound of metal rubbing metal, the sense of progress, the movement of pistons, valves, sprockets, gears, cams and axles, rotors, wheels, the chortles of the operators, the passion that comes with accumulating wealth, the sound of coins so effortlessly dropping into the boxes on the machines.

An operator on a machine nearby puts the machine on automatic and steps down to examine the box.

"Look master," the machinist says. "I'm rich. I'll show you, I'll show you, how rich I've become."

He's heard coins clinking, or thinks he has, but when he opens the lid his machine it squeals to a stop. Chunk-a-chunk, chunk-a-chunk, chunk-a-chunk, clunk, clump.

There's nothing in there.

"Wha…! I heard… There must be money there." The machinist quickly closes the box and hops back up and struggles to restart the machine, which he does, then, pla—, pla—, plump, and then a long screech, a thud, and nothing more. "I'll make more money. I'll make it happen. I'm getting rich. I hear it."

The machinist leans forward on the wheel and sobs profusely.

"I didn't mean to look. I really didn't. I won't do it again. I will never, ever look. I'll believe. I'll have faith. Give me another chance."

He buries his head in his arms and cries in his arms. He puts his hands on his eyes and cries towards heaven.

"Another doubter," the Master says as he and Ralph walk away. "If you look too close, the dream disappears. No room for that at the Dollartorium."

The mechanic falls to the ground and sobs violently. He grovels at the Master's feet.

"Poor soul?" Ralph asks. "Did someone steal his money?"

The Money Master steps up to the machine and slams the lid to the box. Ralph catches a glance inside and indeed sees the box is empty. No coins. No bills. Not even an IOU. No nothing.

"He stopped to count his riches. You have to believe," the Master says. "If you don't believe, you won't get rich, and the machinery breaks down. This one will end up in bankruptcy. We banish unbelievers from this place. They are not to be trusted. Good riddance, I say, to all those who doubt."

A squad of caretakers arrive—sycophants, failed students, aspirants, interns on scholarship. They rush down the pathway with stretchers and straightjackets and first aid kits to where the operator lies weeping on the ground.

"There must be money in there," the operator says between his violent sobs, but he is a broken visionary now. "I am a believer now, Mr. Master. I am. I am. I am a billionaire. I was. It's not fair. I've been cheated."

But he offers no resistance, they roll him on a stretcher, then carry him away. His protestations fade as he is carried to a door that leads outside. They open it, push him to fall out and over the wall.

"You can't doubt your dreams, nor count your wealth, not in the Dollartorium," the Master says. "If you do, it disappears. Maybe, just maybe, he never had any wealth. But what is the difference between acting like you do and being truly wealthy? You must keep up appearances. Make others believe. If you think you're rich, you're rich, but if you think you're poor, you're poor. Truth is what you say it is if everyone believes you."

Ralph absorbs all of this, another lesson learned. Now he is ready and eager to begin on his own machine. It all seems so terribly easy.

"And this," the Master says, nodding to the now abandoned machine. "This is your money machine, Ralph. Slightly used, but in good condition. You can now make coins of your own."

Part 5

RECALLING STELLA

It is lunchtime in Kansas, and you find Stella busy at work making and serving delicious corn dogs to the customers who have formed a long line. The line is longer than usual because her father is absent, off to the Dollartorium learning to make money. Phyllis runs the cash register and hands out receipts and change when she has to. You don't mind waiting in line a little bit longer than usual. The corn dogs will be as delicious as they always are. They are made with the same caring hands and from the same breed of pigs.

Business is good today. It is almost too good for the two of them to handle. But Stella and her mother carry on. Stella worries. Like her father, Stella thinks too much.

"Today I'll have two of your corn dogs, please," the next customer in line tells her. "I been thinking about those corn dogs all morning, and I sure am hungry."

Stella wraps and hands him two corn dogs, still warm from its bath in grease.

"Thank you."

"Where's Ralph?' another customer asks.

"Off to school," Stella says. "Learning how to get rich." Stella lacks enthusiasm for her father's venture. She wipes the sweat from her brow and pulls up another rack of corn dogs from the grease.

"Oh, dear," the customer says. "I hope you all don't get too rich too quick and stop making these wonderful corn dogs. You all make them just about as good as any corn dog can be made." He has hardly paid for his lunch before he squirts on some mustard and takes his first bite.

"I told Father not to go," Stella says to you, the next customer in line. "I feel there will be trouble in all this. 'Daddy,' I said. 'Stick with making corn dogs.' But Daddy is too kind to fight off temptation, nor strong enough not to do what Mother wants. Mother has been completely taken in by some fast-talking dude on television who promised her and everyone infinite riches. How can we all be rich? And if he has a secret on how to do it, why is he selling it instead of getting rich himself? Father should be here, doing what he loves, and doing what he is loved for doing."

"I could eat a hundred of these corn dogs, my dear," you say. "But I'll just take two today, thank you." You get them and then move on to napkins and garnish, then on down the line to pay.

With all the extra work her father's absence requires, Stella barely has time enough to think, much less get angry or tired. She doggedly cooks corn dogs, one rack after another, and serves them up to her beloved customers.

"You see them dipped," she likes to say, "you know they're fresh."

The line seems endless on days when one of the three of them are absent.

"Can I have extra mustard?" the next customer asks.

"Of course, of course." And she hands over the bottle of

mustard.

It is not just the work that concerns Stella so. She also worries how half of the country has fallen for the pitch that one only works to get rich. To them, anyone who is not getting rich is misguided, and, if you are not rich already, you are a failure, just like the half so happy to be poor. Not trying to get rich is, after all, the next thing to being on welfare.

"I told him he does not need to be someone he is not," Stella says to the next customer in line. She shakes the corn dog at them to make her point. "No one needs more than what they need. Trouble comes from wanting more than your own fair share, and those who get that create less for those who have little enough to begin with," she says, startling the gentleman next in line. "Success," Stella continues, "is finding ways to be content with sharing the bounty for us all. Anything less is selfish accumulation."

"I'm sure that's true," says the next man in the line. He owns the local hardware store and has ordered up a dozen corn dogs for the crew he has at work.

But Stella stops to acknowledge the next customer, a special one, a young girl who is here today for the first time. The line slows down as Stella asks the little one to pick the prettiest corn dog she sees hanging on the rack.

"They're all quite good," Stella says, but she knows that the corn dog will be all the better if the young girl chooses it. She picks a fresh one.

"Ah, my dearest, you've picked the best corn dog I ever made. You've got an eye for corn dogs. I hope you love this one and that you come back soon to try another."

The line moves on, and Stella's thoughts resume of her

father and her fears for him.

"I do suppose having more money could make things a little better," Stella says to the next in line. "Don't you suppose?"

The next customer nods, not really knowing the question she has been asked.

"If someone has more money than they need, I suppose they can give to those without, but isn't charity just another form of selfishness? Let the rich alleviate their guilt by not taking more than they need. We do not need to create a desperate class so the rich can pity them and gloat over their own accumulations."

"Do you have fries?" she asks. Stella has not seen this customer before. Perhaps she's from out of town and has come some long, long way to get a famous Corny Doo.

"We don't, good madam. We only serve our corn dogs."

"No onion rings?"

"We don't do onion rings," she says. "We just do Corny Doos."

The line moves on. It seems to stretch out the door and down the sidewalk endlessly. Time passes quicker with Stella lost in thought and as she argues, much like her father does with his philosophy.

"I love my father," she goes on. "He works hard and does as well as anyone. But I suppose he could be tempted by vast riches, as easily as could we all. Like many others, he might take comfort in thinking growing rich is a substitute for goodness. There's so much bad news in the world these days. So many advertisements that demand we change, or spend, or become something that we aren't. I worry anyone can be driven to desperation in this desperate culture. Even in a world as lovely as ours is, who can't be overcome by pain and yearning to grow unfeeling? We are all too easily taught to fear so much by those who sell us goods, and in such a state who could not come to think of money as an answer?"

"I'd like a foot-long corn dog, please."

"We have one size, good sir, that's all, but you can put two of them together, and that'd be a foot or so in length."

Stella smiles, and she sells two, having discovered once again how easy it is for two people who want different things to come to a solution that pleases both.

"We've been put to sleep," she says to the next customer in line. "We've barely stayed awake. We've fueled our lives with Burger Kings and dream of Frosted Flakes. Someone's trained us to smoke cigarettes and made us call it pleasure. To get drunk on killer alcohol and call it socializing. They say that we should fight and win. They say that competition is what it's about. We believe we'll never have enough, so we should seek more all the time. And we've come to think that truth is false and that is not a crime."

Stella vigorously impales fresh hot dogs on sticks, then dips, and dips again, and dips again. Then drops the lot into the grease, which foams again.

"They've turned us against each other, haven't they?" she says to the next customer.

"Oh, yes," the customer says, licking his lips as he eyes the corn dog Stella hands him.

"If we don't see our obligations to each other, we all drown," she says.

The line shuffles along. "Corn dog." "Corn dog." "Two,

please." "Thank you." Stella grows sad, but at last she sees the line will soon be ending. Few customers remain, and the lunch rush is nearly over.

"We should listen to each other, shouldn't we?" she says. The last customer of the day looks up and nods.

"End the endless greed and wake up to better selves."

Then the last customer has been served. Stella knows she has thought too much today to not think it's time for change. Her heart is breaking, and she is full of intent. It's time to act. She takes off her apron and her hat, washes her hands, turns down the gas that heats the grease pot, and, with a wordless kiss to her mother, turns the sign to 'closed' outside, and locks the door, trusting her mother this time to clean up all the mess.

STELLA GOES A-CALLING

We followed Ralph on this trail before. Now we follow Stella as she looks to find her father and keep him from falling into the clutches of the Money Master. It has been a long and arduous journey for Stella, but at last at midday she arrives where the gilded arches and heavy wooden doors mark the entrance to the Dollartorium. She pounds the knocker on the door.

"Let me in," she says. "I want my father! What are you doing to him in there? Open up!"

She peers through the slit in the door and sees a long vast hallway lined with statues of the Money Master and other gods of fraud and embezzlement. Well, there are no other gods; just the Money Master in various guises.

"Someone, open this door!" Stella cries out.

Stella will not be ignored. She is not leaving without her father.

"Who's out there?" comes a voice from inside. It is the cautious Sycophant in its (or hers, or his) low voice. It peers out through the narrow slit.

"I need my father. We have pigs to slaughter and corn dogs to stuff before tomorrow. Who are you?"

"I'm busy," the Sycophant says. "I'm studying business

plans. Risk and margins, and hedges, futures. Very difficult stuff. Very difficult, indeed. It takes a genius, you know, to understand all this. Not a place for amateurs. Now where was I before you interrupted me? Oh, yes. If the government drops the discount rate, the best way to make money is to …"

Stella keeps pounding. Frustrated, the Sycophant gives up and opens the door.

"That's the second time this week I've lost my place in my studies. Earlier it was some little maker of corn dogs who had to come in. Who just had to come in. Can just anyone feel they can come into this place? Can the rich get no peace?" it says. "Once upon a time this place was more exclusive. A higher class of students. Back when I first arrived."

"That was my father who bothered you," Stella says. "My father is the one who makes corn dogs. What have you done to him? Where is he now? It's time for him to come home and do some real and meaningful work."

She looks left and right, pushes past it, then heads down the hallway to the waiting room, past elevators and escalators, and doors to the left and right.

At first the Sycophant is stunned, but then it follows her closely, all the while complaining, "You don't belong here. You don't have a ticket. You must pay a fee. Who said you could come? If you have the fee, though, we can work something out. Yes, we can work something out. How much money do you have?"

Stella enters the reception room and rings the bell on the desk several times. Ding! Ding! The Sycophant darts around to the far side of the desk.

"Do you have a reservation?" the Sycophant asks.

It picks up a pen and opens the book to see if her name is on any list.

"And why are you here?" the Sycophant continues. "Why don't you go? I don't see your name. I don't know who you are. Bother someone who has the time to be bothered. I don't care who you are. I'm richer than you are. Go away."

"Ralph is my father," Stella says. "He came here earlier today, or at least this is where he was headed. We need him back at work. He runs the Doggery back in town and we can't do without him. He's about this high, this round," she says, waving her hands to demonstrate his features. "He wears a paper hat to keep corn meal out of his hair when he works. And an apron so his pants don't get dirty. Mother insists. And most likely there is cornmeal dust on his shoes. And he would be carrying a book of Plato."

"Ah, Plato. He's that one," the Sycophant says. "Yes, he's here with the Money Master, and they're busy. Too busy for you. But, frankly, I'm sick of them both, of their corn dogs and having to stick my bare butt up in the air to applaud, and of these hot air balloons which are so yesterday. It's all 'Ralph this' and 'Ralph that.' I should never have let him in. Everyone wants to be a billionaire. Find him, please, and take him, and good luck with your corn dogs."

"I will," Stella begs, "if you'll just show me the way."

The lobby is crowded with the people Ralph had also seen on his arrival. The crowd glances about here and there, pretending not to look, pretending to read newspapers, gossip, drink coffee, or pose as if they are waiting for someone important. The grandeur, those stuffed chairs, the burbling fountains, goods sold in fancy stores, shiny shoes on all feet, clever but useless things to buy, such vacuousness surrounds our poor Stella.

The Sycophant twists its short, flat head and stares at Stella from the corner of its eye. The Sycophant may have failed to master the Money Master's art—as indeed none of these hangers-about have fully done—but it knows enough to keep its eye out for the chance to turn what little authority it has into a bit of cash. It senses that in Stella.

"There is work to do at home," Stella says. "Pigs need feeding, corn needs shucking, and a hundred corn dogs need to be dipped in grease. Heaven knows I miss him."

"Oh," the Sycophant says. "We are all management here. Nobody works. But I think I know this fellow. A fast learner, he is. He did some sessions today on firing someone's ass, and hiring someone, selling something, planning something. He was …" Then it pauses. "He's good, for sure, but no better than me. I can fire someone, too. Just like that, and for no reason. I suppose he thinks he's better than I. That he and his corn dogs make him better than us? Maybe he thinks that. Maybe he does. Well, does he?"

The Sycophant stands, then it leaps to the desk and bends down, its face in Stella's.

"My father is a good man," Stella says. "He works with us. He has no one to fire but my mother and I."

"Slaughtering pigs, indeed," the Sycophant says. "No man who wants to be rich would waste his time shucking corn, I'll have you know, or would cook hot dogs in grease, or would sweat dipping dogs in corn batter. I don't think so. I don't think so. No, I don't."

This conversation has caught the attention of everyone in the foyer, for among them, even in a short time, Ralph has become some sort of hero. Many try, but few make it through the Master's sessions with such skill. Fewer still are rewarded with money machines such as Ralph now has.

"There's nothing wrong with work," Stella says. "Work done honestly and with care. Good can only come from good."

"That's corn dog morality!" The Sycophant returns to its numbers and ink with a snort.

Many in the waiting room snort out laughter as well.

"You and your type make me sick," the Sycophant continues. "You do. Really do. You really do. Well, here's what I'll do. I'll show you Ralph if it's still Ralph you'll see when you see him. We'll take the tour. See his machine. See him running it. The latest model, the latest features. Overdrive. High-speed printing. It's a honey, it is. I should have it. With it he can price something high over here and lower over there—borrowing all the cash he wants to cover his assets. It can minimize or maximize the very same assets, both at the same time, good for borrowing and lending, and reducing one's taxes. It converts dollars to shekels, piasters to yuans, pesos to gold—"

It yawns.

"And from Bitcoin to Green Stamps with the flick of a switch."

It is jealous. Anyone can see that.

"There is no need for him to be doing that," Stella says. "We need him at the Corny Doo Doggery. We need him to make corn dogs, so people don't go hungry."

"Corny Doo, Corny Don't, I don't care about hunger," the Sycophant says. "Do you? I say, let's be done with corn dogs altogether and let the poor be hungry somewhere else." The Sycophant leaps off the desk and takes Stella's hand. "Let us be done with Ralph, too. He's been nothing but trouble. The Master has no time for me now that he has that dog dipper about. He has no time left to teach me anything. I'm going nowhere anymore. I have sat at this desk, at the door, at his feet, and I wait, and I wait, and nothing happens. Not since this pig killer arrived. Let's go find him. Then you can take him away from our business here."

The Sycophant points down another corridor towards the room of machines.

"Follow that to the end, then at the end," the Sycophant says, "take any door out."

Stella heads down the hallway. For a short while it follows Stella, its head on her shoulder as she follows a path as complex as roots in the ground. In the distance, she hears machinery.

"Father!" she calls out. "Father! Father!"

"I once was a teacher," the Sycophant whispers. "You wouldn't know it now. But I made no money. So, I went into politics. But that was too hard. So, I become a lobbyist. But you still end up working, a graft here, a graft there. So, I came to the Dollartorium to study the business of doing business without working at all, and now I buy lobbyists, politicians, and anyone else. I was doing quite well. I was on my way. I should be on television by now. But your father arrived …"

"Father!" Stella calls out. "Father! Father!"

"Your father has changed," the Sycophant says. "You'll see that. Yes, you will. He's changed. He's set his mind on riches. He can never be poor again. He has to make money. He has to make more. Once you've seen glitter, your life sparkles gold. You can't lose what you've got once you've got it, you see. Once you think you do, it's everything. You can become alcoholic, schizophrenic, hook yourself on dope; pop pills, be a crook, be a thief, or a politician; you can forsake all reason, shed morals like leaves, promise voters all they want, buy your path out of prison. But you can never be poor once you've tasted true wealth. You can't stand it."

"Have you ruined my father?" Stella says. She has stopped, turned, and put her finger in its face. "That's what you do here, isn't it? I know."

"One ruins one's own self, if ruin it is. We just helped him along. And once his machine gets going … Go find him, my dear. Save your father, stop the machine, take him home to the pig farm, back to his corn dogs. I'd like that a lot. Then I'll take his machine. His machine will be mine. Then the Master will have time for this dearly beloved. The fewer we are, the more I am wanted and the richer I'll grow."

The Sycophant opens a door. Before them stretches the vast array of machines and machinists. The hum of the machines. The shouts and screams of businessmen doing business. The smell of human exhaust as wealth is created.

Stella goes in, and with a chortle from it who stands behind her, the door closes.

OH, JEALOUS HEART

A control module hangs by wires from the dome above the factory where the entrepreneurs on their machines are creating their wealth. From inside the module, one can survey the entire floor of the Dollartorium. There are controls for temperature, power, light, and sensors to measure the efforts and results of the machinists at work. Monitors and blinking instruments survey all the activities below. This control module is the Sycophant's lair, and it is now alone in the booth, spying on machinists as they run their machines, and on Ralph whom the Sycophant thinks doesn't belong, and on this Stella who has sneaked in and will discover the truth. It should never have let Ralph enter the Dollartorium, nor his daughter who's here for a rescue. It doesn't think Ralph knows how to run his machine, how to make wealth flow from it, and anyway, this maker of corn dogs doesn't deserve to have such a thing. Not like Sycophant does. Well, it has a plan to steal this machine by letting this virtuous one discover the truth.

Ralph pumps the pedals on his machine, pulling levers, turning wheels, looking comfortable at the controls as if he has been operating this equipment for years, not hours, and as if he has already accumulated a fortune. He doesn't dare look to see if he had made much money. He hasn't, but he hopes, he believes. Remember what happened to the previous operator. To attempt to prove what you believe only implies your lack of faith. Still, Ralph knows he has made money. He knows it. For sure. The Master has promised him, so it must be true. Ralph is whistling as he works. It is a Disney tune.

"I am not happy," the Sycophant says to itself as it looks down from the sky booth. It flies from one control panel to another, pushing, pulling, controlling, going from one set of lights to another, staring at this screen, then that screen, then puts a quarter in the slot and pulls the lever. Is he lucky? Is he lucky? Do the gods of chance love him? The wheels go round like a slot machine. No. No. Yes. He doesn't win.

"I'm gonna win. I'm gonna win. Sometime I'm gonna win," the Sycophant says. Another quarter. Another tug. The wheel stops. Yes. No. Nothing. He doesn't win.

"Next time," he says.

Another quarter. He pulls the handle.

"I'm gonna win. I'm gonna win. I'm gonna win."

Bonus. Bonus. Nothing.

The Sycophant kicks the machine, then returns to spying on Ralph.

"That fool," Sycophant says to itself. "Pretending to be a 'businessman.' Corn dogs. He's a born worker, that's all, like many others, raised that way, acts that way, does that way. Wages are for the slaves, that's what I say!"

It slithers about the booth. Hundreds of financial types work their machines below. Whatever they are doing, to whatever their effect, it emits a sense of confidence as it slinks about.

"A 'maker of corndogs,'" it snarls. "Why does the Master

like Ralph so much? The Master should love me more," it thinks. "He should have given me that machine. I love him. Yes, I do. But he loves this maker of corn dogs, instead, and he is teaching him our tricks. How to swindle. How to cheat. What's the business world coming to? I say, no. I say, no. I say, no, no, no … Me."

It pauses. It puts another quarter in and pulls the lever. No. No. Bonus.

"I won't have it. That machine. It's mine. Yes, yes. I should be next. I should get rich. I should be the one to sit at his right hand. And hold his hat. And hold his cane. Be with him on television. I was wrong to let that Ralph get in this place at all."

The Sycophant can also spy on Stella as she wanders about in the crowd below, up and down aisles, between booths and machines, operators, deal makers, deal breakers, and money exchangers, frantically calling out for her father. She looks determined and unafraid, threading her way through the operators, hustlers, and crooks. Some try to sell her goods, or this scheme, or that thing, all planning to get rich by finding enough fools, but Stella walks by, not even tempted.

"Father!" she cries out. She fears what can happen to him in a place like this. She fears what might have happened already.

The Sycophant hears her, even in its module hanging from the dome.

"Were there ever two so horribly nice people as these?" the Sycophant says. "These two … these two such gentle people. They make me sick. They're out of place. They should be punished. If they were dogs, I would kick them. If they were corn dogs, I would ..."

It focuses its cameras on Ralph. A metallic clatter comes from Ralph's machine. It could be coins falling into the box on the end. It could be pistons of the machine that rattle if the oil's low.

"See?" the Sycophant says. "He doesn't know how to run it. I knew it. I knew it. He's a danger to us all. I would not have let him in."

"I wonder how much wealth I have created already," Ralph is saying softly as he operates the machine. "I'll buy a pool. No, first I'll buy a great big car. No, first I'll take my dear wife on a vacation someplace fancy. Then she'll love me." His smile shows Ralph gets more pleasure spending his fortune than earning it. He pumps the machine even faster, then faster. But others are running their machines fast, too. As stationary as they are, everyone on these Dollartorium machines is certain they are getting somewhere.

"I should be on that," the Sycophant says. "His money should all be mine. If I'm not getting filthy rich, no one should be getting filthy rich. At least not him. I hate him. I do. He shouldn't be here. I'm better than he is. I'm smarter than he is. I'm greedier than anyone else can ever be. And I was here first. I've served the boss longer. I've served him better. Yes, I love him. There will never be another Master like the Master. I'll do anything for him. Especially if he gives me money. Which is to say, I'll do all I can do, if the Master asks, and more for lovely lucre. So, why not me? No, I shouldn't have let this corn dog maker in."

It looks down at Ralph and scowls. It's angry, and here in this chaotic room, hate is a dangerous thing.

"Of all of those here on their machines, I'm the worst there ever was. And here the worst's the best. I fetch, I lie, I cheat for a buck, and I help the rich get richer. I keep the Master's phony books for him. I fix his stupid taxes—so he pays no taxes, never has, and that's pretty good for a man so rich. I even let the Master owe me money."

The Sycophant paces around the control room. The angrier it gets, the better it begins to feel. It creates a plan, and it nearly bursts into song.

"I'm a dirty little, rotten, stinking, smelly, sleazy rat," it says. "I'm a rotten little wretch with all the cunning of a cat. I can cheat, and steal, and rob, and kill, and stab you in the back. I'm despicable and slimy with a heart that's cold and black."

It hugs one of the slot machines, then kicks it. Coins pour out. The wheels turn. Win. Win. Win!

"It matters less to me if I'm your dearest friend. If you got any money, then I'll steal it in the end. And if, you little fuckers, think you're on a happy ride, remember me, the Sycophant, waits on the other side ..."

It stares at the camera. Down there Ralph looks so happy. Ha! How it hates that. Stella, so concerned about her silly father, looks so innocent. Ha! That will change. It will change it. It's going to start to change things now.

"I'm a dirty little, rotten, stinking, smelly, sleazy rat. I'm a rotten little wretch with all the cunning of a cat."

WE MUST BELIEVE

For the first time in his life, Ralph feels in control of his destiny. In the Dollartorium, atop this new machine, he feels invincible. He is convinced his newfound skills will bring him a new life and vast riches. He sits on his machine and pedals as fast as he can, or as fast as the gears, levers, and his legs allow. He's in a hurry to make his fortune and get home before dinner.

He is eager, and he believes.

"This is it," he tells himself. "This is what it's all about. What have I been doing all my life? I've wasted years getting nowhere. Making corn dogs, for heaven's sake!"

He says that with distaste.

"The world is mine now that I have a machine for making money. A machine that will get me somewhere. Money. Money. Where have you been all my life?"

Pump, pump, pump. He pats the machine where a horse's neck would be if were it a horse.

Faster and faster. He pushes buttons, turns on lights, pulls levers, watches dials, pedals, absorbed.

"This baby is certainly a real honey," Ralph mutters.

It runs so smoothly, as one hopes a new machine will do.

Maybe it is even smoother than that, smoother than he expected, and faster than he dared hope, had he known what to expect or to hope the thing worked at all. Okay, it's a surprise, but that's a good thing, too, as long as money is the end result.

The machine he is working on is the super-duper money model. Not the silver, not the gold, but the platinum model. He has much to learn. If he adjusts the monitors, he can see other people anywhere, see what they are doing, where they are going, how they think, how they feel, how they will vote, and with some adjusting he can even tweak some things and change those votes. For a fee, of course. The machine will tell him what to say with this group of people, and what other things to say with that other group of people, to get them angry, or hungry, or up out of their chairs with an ax handle to go out and change the world. Or to buy whatever he has to sell. He can get them to march with a torch in their hands. With other adjustments, Ralph can see their thoughts, their dreams, their histories, the patterns of their lives, and their habits—good and bad. Not that he cares what they think or dream, but knowing that allows him to control what they do. It allows him to make what he sells fit their dreams. These machines are tied into infinite data collected in the past, data that is still being collected now, on them, on him, on everyone, and knowing that, using that, those thoughts, and desires, he can chart the part to make the money flow his way.

Pump, pump, pump.

Those stupid oafs, he thinks. He focuses his machine on some unknowing fool he sees in the monitor, and Ralph makes the old fart dance a jig. He makes another buy a pillow. Another he makes hate his own children for the dangerous books they read and buy more illustrated books of fairies and goblins and creatures of fantasy. The more data fed into his machine, the more it learns, the more he's in control of other people's lives. How fun is that?

And the more he's in control, the more money flows his way.

He can learn who has the money. He can learn what who wants more than they have and will pay hard cash for it. Who will fail, who will go broke, and who will pay him anyway. Who might succeed; who is a threat; who needs to learn a lesson. Who will sell what they have for less than it's worth which he can then buy, then sell for more than its worth, to someone who doesn't know the difference, and make a tidy profit. How much will they pay? Who bought what from whom and when, how much they paid, and even when will they need a replacement part for something he sold them months ago, so, just at the moment a replacement part is needed, he sends them an ad to remind them. How much he can sell and what he can charge? How much he can make if he creates a shortage. How rich can he be if he wants to be richer? And how quick will that all happen?

Meanwhile, no one he watches knows he is watching. Isn't that the beauty of this money machine.

Pump, pump, pump.

This is money. Money. Money. And money's real—that's what counts—a joy to feel it accumulate, even if it is invisible, mere totals of wealth kept in the box beneath Ralph's butt. He sits on it. He likes to tell people how much there is. He is certain he hears the coins rattling about.

"Riches," Ralph tells himself. It's there. He knows it's

there. He has a malicious grin. "I am rich. I am special. I am good."

Pump, pump, pump.

He thinks about the future but knows nothing except that all his desires will be fulfilled. That is certain. Desires he knows and desires he has yet to desire. This fabulous wealth is a constant surprise. Riches will bring their own appetite for riches.

He will calculate his wealth, how rich he is, how rich he'll become, how poor he was, how poor he'll never be again. His life before, what a waste, his helplessness, so much like these fools he sees on his monitors. He knows them better than they know themselves. Motes in the sunlight on a late afternoon—slow-falling dust in the light. Pretty, but pathetic. Like little corn dog makers, pitiful, ignorant. He smirks. It's good to recall he was once so humble, because it makes the distance he has come all the greater.

"This machine's a beaut," Ralph says.

Pump, pump, pump.

He plays with switches, buttons, lights, and sings songs of happiness and good times. He closes his eyes, hits a button and, voila, another transaction occurs in the world, then he hears, or imagines, a clink in the bucket, a quarter perhaps, or a silver dollar, or—who knows—perhaps just a slug.

The Master quietly floats above the machines on his hot air balloon and lands on a pathway near Ralph.

"Ralph," he says. "You look so happy now."

"I'm rich," Ralph says. "And growing richer."

Ralph pats the metal box wherein is stored his happiness. He pedals faster, faster, to show off to the Master.

Pump, pump, pump.

"Slow down, Ralph," the Master says. He has a worried look. These things take time to learn and to control. I've seen them get out of hand, and, 'poof', the whole neighborhood is broke again."

"This baby's a wonder," Ralph says. "Yes, she is."

Metal on metal, wealth accumulates inside his wonder machine. Ralph can feel it as it grows, yes, he can, growing bigger, growing warmer, there between his loins.

The Master shrugs and floats away on his balloon. There is not much one can do to control a man who has stumbled onto greed. An hour later he floats by to check on Ralph's progress again. The Master is proud Ralph has taken to his new status with such a flourish. Ralph waves at the Master in his balloon and smiles.

"You have learned much, Ralph," the Master says. He drops a rope to the earth which minions pull gently down. "But you still can learn a little bit more. There are always new buttons to push," the Master says. "Tricks to learn. Strategies to test out. How to complain so one never has to pay an invoice. There's a whole world of legal strategies. How to sue the bastards who think you owe them money—lawyers, contractors, and other fuddy-duddies—so they leave you alone so you can do what you want. How to find a lawyer who'll do what you want. God, and then there's politics and all the politicians! Running for office, that's perhaps the best scam of all, because who has more money than the government? A workshop on that may take a whole week."

The Master sits on Ralph's machine and gently pushes Ralph aside with his butt. The Master takes control.

"Let me show you some tricks, and a few shortcuts," he says, pointing to the funnel at the mouth of the machine. "This is for input."

Pump, pump, pump.

"Yes," Ralph says. "I see that."

"And this," he says, "for output," pointing to a pipe sticking out the rear.

Ralph sniffs the air above the rear of the machine.

"That smells like …"

"It is, it is," the Master says. "And isn't it sweet? It's money, Ralph. Good in any store. Accepted throughout the world. If you're not used to it, hold your nose until you are."

Pump, pump, pump.

"Do you hear the coins dropping out?" the Master asks.

Ralph shakes his head.

"Oh, false alarm," the Master says.

Pump, pump, pump.

"Maybe we should put something in," Ralph says.

"Yes, yes," the Master says. "Today let's give her a pork belly or two. I sense an epidemic among the pigs. A shortage of food is so profitable."

With a wave of the hand, minions appear, all bearing an armload of pork bellies. Of course, no one sees anything there, since pork belly doesn't really exist.

"Throw them in," the Master says.

"There is nothing to throw in," Ralph says.

"The pork bellies," the Master says.

The sly Sycophant who has been lurking around Ralph's

machine all day jumps on the platform and feeds the machine all the pork bellies the minions offer up to him. The Money Master kicks the machine. It grinds a bit, then grinds away. It's grinding something.

Pump, pump, pump.

A quarter drops out of the exhaust pipe. Or it sounds like a quarter has dropped out anyway. Maybe it's a slug. Ralph fishes it out. It's a shiny thing.

"There. You see? No muss. No fuss," the Master says. "Just money. You're becoming a businessman, Ralph. Now, I'll take that and leave you to fill your own coffer with riches."

Ralph most reluctantly gives up the coin—or the slug if it's a slug—and, as the Master steps into his balloon, Ralph mounts his machine once again, eager to make some money of his own.

"I can do it. I can do it," Ralph says. He is eager to resume his pedaling. "I know I can. I know I can."

Pump, pump, pump.

The minions surround him, all waiting to see Ralph's output. Ralph is pumping, the Syc is frowning, and for all that effort, or imagination, nothing changes. Ralph pumps faster.

"There, I feel it," Ralph says. "Don't you feel it? Wealth is happening. There," he says. "In the bucket. Input more bellies, please. More. And more."

Ralph pats the bin beneath his butt, trusting it is filling up with the wealth he is creating, and, as he pumps faster, faster, lights begin flashing, and there are whistles, noise, and—so we are led to suppose—money trickling in. Money. Money.

Pump, pump, pump.

Our dear Ralph. Little Ralph, growing richer. Lately of the corn dog trade. Once a working man and rather happy. Now in a silk hat, pumping wildly, in a frenzy.

REUNION

Ralph is obsessing on his new machine when Stella finally spots him. A crowd has surrounded Ralph and eggs him on. 'More and more!' they shout, and 'Harder, harder, faster, faster!' which is not hard to get poor Ralph to do, as he relishes the moment and the spotlight. He pumps away, there is the sound of metallic clatter, be it coins or the machine growing unstable. From time to time, he clasps his hands above his head and stands and bows to the crowd. Then he hurriedly gets back to pumping out more cash.

"Father!" Stella shouts.

Her voice barely carries over the crowd, but it is too soft to get Ralph's attention.

"Father!"

She climbs up on the machine and shakes poor Ralph out of his frenzy.

"Stella," Ralph says as he recognizes her. His eyes are wide, and he has a look Stella has never seen before. "Look at me, Stella. I'm making money now."

Ralph holds up a rock.

"That's a rock," Stella says. "That's not money."

"But it is money, my dear," Ralph says. His voice is soft

and condescending. He does love her. "Because I say it is money, and that makes it so. It's like a quarter or a dollar. But this rock could also be worth more now because I say it's worth more. They do it with the Bitbucks. Why not with rocks? Here," he says, and he puts the rock in Stella's hand. "I say, 'It's worth a dollar,' and it is. And thus, I've made more than it cost me for the rock. And isn't the world all the richer for the deal? Or at least, aren't I all the richer for it? So ..." And here Ralph pauses, looks at the stone, turns it over in one hand and strokes his chin with the other. "I say it's worth ... at least a dollar."

"How can that be worth a dollar, Daddy? It's a rock. Unless you are going to build something and need a rock ... Oh, Father. You are drowning in delusions."

"And now," he says, his eyes brightening, "I say it's worth ten dollars. How's that?! I've made nine dollars, and I didn't do a thing. Here. You can have this rock, my dear. Go buy yourself something frilly and foolish. There's more where that's come from."

Ralph remounts his machine.

"Oh, Father ..."

Tears well up in Stella's eyes.

"Come home with me," she says. "We have real work to do, and bills to pay that have to be paid with real money."

"This is my home now, Stella. It is my new home. And these," he says, waving to the crowd. "These are my new friends."

Again, he clasps his hands above his head and bows to the crowd who have gathered on all sides of his machine. They go wild, chanting 'Money! Money! Money!"

"Daddy," Stella says. "This place has driven you mad. There is nothing here. This is only a rock!"

"Oh, fuddy duddy," he says and starts up his machine. "Money, art, truth, those things are only what we say they are. A painting that could have sold for a hundred dollars a decade ago might sell for a million today, and what's changed? Not the painting. Just someone's thinking that it's worth that much. Things are worth what we say they're worth. And I ask you, dearest daughter, what's Good? Well, I'll be the judge of that. Now, let me get down to business."

Ralph sits in the seat and begins turning on switches, and dials, and rotating the wheels.

"We'll put our pork bellies in here—or ideas, or sweat, or a raft of fresh foreclosures or mortgages, whatever you got, anything that's really nothing, but can be redeemed for cash. And we grind it up …"

Ralph fiddles with the input, then pats the output, sniffs the air, then sits again on his machine. He pulls a level, wheels go 'round, and the crowd groans with anticipation. Two quarters—or maybe slugs, you don't really know because you don't dare look—drop out the rear and onto the ground with a plop. Ralph stands again and makes bows around to all the crowd.

"What about corn dogs, Daddy? What about our customers?"

"Corn dogs, you say! How sweet. But silly. Corn dogs are all sweat and work. Pork and corn, just to make money when it's much easier to make promises. And who can be hurt with a few words? But if you eat a corn dog too fast …"

"You might as well be gambling as running that

machine," she says, "for all the good it does the world."

"Exactly, dear. You're getting it now."

"What do you think you are doing here? It's nothing, which comes to nothing. Daddy …"

She implores him, but Ralph is absorbed in pedaling his machine.

Pump, pump, pump.

"I got a plan, Stella, and it is worth a lot of money. Okay, here it is. We push down wages everywhere, so even wives and kids must work two jobs to make ends meet, see? Kids work, wives work, and they don't see each other or have time to talk, so we sell them phones and make them pay every month, and they work so long they don't have time to cook, so we sell them fast food, and they get fat, so we sell them diet food, and special walking shoes, see? Shoes! So they walk! Like they can't walk without special shoes. Or exercise without belonging to a gym! There you have it, a million consumers working to pay so they can overwork. We take a piece of all that."

"Daddy. That's the way things are already."

"Oh. Okay. So while they rest, we'll sell them on … television! No rational thoughts, no books, no newspapers, no conversations, only television. Then we'll put ideas in their heads about things they don't have, about things they want, about how bad they are and things they need, things we sell. We'll call it … advertising."

"Daddy. They already do that. Most have big screens, too. And cable. And streaming and …"

"I suppose they already have couches with those little beer holders …"

"Widely available. Hugely popular."

"Okay. Okay. So … Sex. Yes, sex. That's good. Sex and fear. We'll sell them sex and fear. Show them so many guns they have to buy guns to feel safe. Keep them constantly in fear. Politics and television, blogs and internet media, twenty-four hours a day. Crime, and murder, war, and guns, politics … and sex. Tell them, no matter what else they may be doing they should be having sex."

"Uh, Daddy …"

When Ralph looks at her, she nods.

"Already done?" Ralph says. "Well, how about a news station that tells them twenty-four/seven they are being cheated, robbed, and taxed to death, that immigrants are invading our country, raping our women, socialists cutting into our God-given social security, forcing their communist health insurance on us …"

"Fox News."

"Oh. Okay. Okay. We'll keep them so anxious they won't go anywhere but the malls and fast-food restaurants, too fearful to cook they order from Door Dash. Scared to go out the door, they order online. Scare them to death, so they only have sex home alone, where they start to think they feel something …"

"Daddy?"

"Yes, sweetheart?"

"You're touching yourself."

Ralph looks down. He discovers he is.

THE COLLAPSE

So Ralph runs his machine, generating wealth, and more wealth, on, and on, and on, and the machine shivers—it goes so fast! —and strains, almost out of control, then, just when Ralph thinks he might have accumulated enough, all he or anyone might ever need, Ralph sighs, but then collapses. He slumps over the wheel on his machine, and Stella climbs up to revive him. The machine sighs, too, and slows to a stop.

"I knew this would happen," Stella says. She helps him off the machine and lies him on the ground.

"This place is unnatural for anyone but the most hard-hearted, money-minded, narcissistic of fools," Stella says. "More healthy people need a touch of reality, some time in nature, or they will lose themselves to the demons of money and greed."

"Reality?" Ralph says. He slurs his words. His eyes are half open and they wander. He is dazed. "Nature?"

"Nature is both kind and real, and we need to remind ourselves there is a world of truth that we can touch and that we are part of something quite real and greater than we are. Otherwise, we float along on selfish dreams and delusions and forget we not only share the earth, oceans, and sky, but we are part of them, and nothing more. Remove ourselves from that, and we are suddenly alone, filled with an emptiness. And empty, we grow afraid. And that's no way to live your life to its very best."

Ralph lays flat on his back and looks up at the sky. Of course, there is no sky here, only images of the Master painted on the dome.

"Sky?" he says weakly. Ralph is stunned, incoherent. He looks around, not understanding.

"You need to get some fresh air," Stella says. "Let's go home."

Now that Ralph has abandoned his machine, the Sycophant sees his opportunity and slinks through the crowd and slithers aboard Ralph's machine, happily wriggling onto the seat.

"Look at me! Look at me!" the Sycophant says, as it fires up Ralph's engine once again. "I can do it! I can do it! I can run it. I can run it better. I can make more money, too."

The machine roars alive and, after a few chugs, the wheels begin to turn. There is a clanking louder than before, a heavy wheezy pumping, as the cylinders fire inside.

"Others can go make corn dogs, thank you," it says. "I'm going to make some money!"

"Let's leave this place, Daddy," Stella says, holding Ralph's arm and helping him stand. He rubs his head. He's had a concussion. "Mother is home, running the store alone, and tomorrow will be time to make more corn dogs for our friends."

"Corn dogs?" Ralph says. Ralph slowly becomes aware of where he is.

The crowd is preoccupied with their new hero, the

Sycophant. Even above the roar of their approval, they hear the clinking of metal falling from the rear pipe.

"I am the best of us," it says. "I will be the richest."

"Money, money, money, money," the mob begins to chant. They are a frightening lot, and angry. They shake their fists at nothing in particular, but they are urged on by the Sycophant.

"Money?" Ralph repeats.

Ralph's machine, now run by the Sycophant, is going faster and faster. There is no stopping it. No governing its greed. No slowing down the sound of coins—or perhaps slugs, how can we know what we cannot see? —flowing into the box attached to the rear of the machine. But then fewer coins are heard dropping. Then fewer. Then even fewer. And at last, only a very few. Then finally at long last there is no more clinking, but the machine still runs, faster and faster.

"What's wrong?" the Sycophant asks. It kicks the machine as if that might fix it. "Look at me! Look at me! I can do it. I can do it." It hops up and down on the platform, opens doors to the engine, the fuel tanks, panels, and then gives what it finds a few tweaks and twists to see what might happen. Then back on the seat.

Pump, kerplump, kerplump-plump.

No matter how hard the Sycophant tries to fix things, tries to make the machine work faster, harder, better, richer, nothing happens. It jumps on it, pulls levers this way and that, as if it knows how this thing works—it doesn't. Not really. The machine is as much a mystery to the Sycophant as it has been to Ralph. It is a new machine, anyway, a new model that does what it is programmed to do—make money—but it also learns from what it does, and then when it's learned what it's learned, it teaches itself to do better, at least do it faster, and smoother, at last making money from money, if on paper, then in ever larger denominations, so the amount grows, not arithmetically, not algebraically, but logarithmically, exponentially, its speed controlled by only itself, to no end, to be more, and then more, and then faster and faster.

So it goes, creating money from metal, then money from paper, then Bitcoins from electrons, and then promises, and dreams, all done must faster and more furious, and more dangerous, until it is at warp speed making nothing from nothing at all. No machine has never created wealth as fast, but this one's now out of control. Anyone can see that, if anyone looks, but no one is looking at the machine at all. They are looking for money, and of course wealth cannot be seen.

The crowd has grown dangerously frenzied.

"Money, money, money, money …"

The Sycophant dances on top of the machine, letting the machine control itself.

"Money is everything," the Sycophant decrees. "Look at me! Look at me!"

Then it hops back down and pedals it, and pedals faster and faster. The wheels turn as it pulls levers here and there, another, then another, in no particular order. Just frantic movement. It is just pretending it knows how this works. It is manic. It is greedy. It pushes buttons. Lights go on; lights go off; lights flicker. No one sees the output, but the coffers surely fill with Bitbucks or whatever the latest form wealth has taken. You must just know wealth is there. You must believe. The crowd believes.

"It's going to explode," Stella says.

"Look at the wealth," the Sycophant says. "Look at me."

"We see," its followers say. "We see." And they are indeed its followers now. They are its greatest fans. Devotees who of course will follow one so successful, so rich. How did it do it? Can we do it, too? Teach us. We want to be like you.

Delusion feeds frenzy.

"Aren't I good? Aren't I good?" the Sycophant says.

The crowd roars back in the affirmative.

"There is nothing here for us," Stella says to her father. "Nothing here we want."

Stella strains to stand her father up, to help him take his first few steps to freedom from this place. The crowd is growing wilder and more dangerous.

"Money is food!" someone shouts from the crowd.

"Money is pleasure!"

"Cash is truth!"

"Cash is sex!"

"God is money."

"We want money."

"Money is meaning."

"Money is money!"

And on and on, but Stella no longer listens, and Ralph remains in a daze.

"Look at me! Look at me!" the Sycophant is shouting. It is the center of attention. It tweaks the gears on the money machine, pushes the buttons, and adjusts the settings, unaware of the growing danger to itself and all the others, perhaps not caring about the risk as long as whatever it is doing results in riches. There is money to be made. It feels it. It believes it. The whole machine begins to shake. The earth beneath begins to shake as well.

"We need to get home to make corn dogs, Daddy."

Ralph is still somewhat in a daze.

"I like corn dogs" Ralph says.

His voice sounds small in all this noise of this hysterical mob.

"Ralph," the Sycophant hollers out. Ralph doesn't hear it. It yells to the crowd, "Stop him. Kill him. He's a fake billionaire. He's a spy. He's a Democrat. He's a socialist. Throw him to his creditors."

Stella keeps Ralph moving, one step at a time, away from this place, away from the Dollartorium and all the fools there, looking for a way to get out of that place.

"I've done it. I've made it work, my very own machine," the Sycophant says. "I'm richer than you. I'm smarter than you. I'm more loved than you will ever be. And richer. Far richer. Perhaps the richest there is."

"Money, money, money …" The crowd does love it.

"Come back, little man!" the Sycophant shouts, surveying the crowd as he searches for Ralph and his daughter. "You work for me now. Come back. Come back! You're fired!"

Ralph and Stella thread their way through the mob. When they are recognized, they are hit, or pushed, or spit at, or shouted down. The mob of would-be billionaires enjoys tantalizing this poor pair as much as the Sycophant does. Because their Sycophant does. They have their new hero, and they want to please it. And they have found the one with the hat and the apron who has taken the place they should have had, the place at the side of the Master. If they had been chosen instead of that fool, they would be rich and gloriously useless.

"Look at me! Look at me!" the Sycophant says, and it slithers about as it wrangles the machine. The machine throws him about, but for now he holds on.

"Money, money, money ..."

"I feel a new world is being born," the Sycophant says. "I feel it in my guts, wealth rising in my belly ..."

The pain bends it over.

"I hear thunder," Stella says softly to her father. She has gotten him away from the crowd, and now she searches the outer walls for a way out of this Dollartorium—a crack in the wall, a door, a window, anything. "We must get out of here quickly."

Finally, she finds it, a new crack in the wall which will serve as a doorway, and they run to crawl through and escape.

Behind them the thunderous sound grows louder. The machine strains and shivers, increasing the instability of the world beneath them.

"Hurry, Father." Stella struggles to wedge herself through the crack. "That lizard is running that thing too fast. It's shaking the whole place to pieces."

When they turn to look back, they see the Sycophant standing on top of the machine and writhing, bent over, aching, holding his gut.

Lightning streaks across the roof of the dome, making more thunder and noise, drowning out for a moment the rumbling that comes from the Sycophant's gut.

"Money is thunder!" the Sycophant says. "And thunder is …"

But its words are caught short. The noise from the machine—the clunking and clattering of metal against metal, of iron banging on iron, of the pumping of pistons, thud, thud, thud, of papers printed and shuffled, deals inked and stamped and dated and notarized, contracts signed and submitted, drowns out the painful cries of the Sycophant.

"Money, money, money, money …" The crowd senses nothing of the coming catastrophe, so enthralled they are with the Sycophant and its money, so frantic at finding the anarchist Ralph. Fights are breaking out in the crowd, guns drawn and aimed threateningly, such is their great hateful joy.

"Hurry, Daddy," Stella says. "We must get home and get to dipping dogs and doing honest, peaceful work."

The crack finally opens wider. The giant walls begin crumbling.

"Corn dogs," Ralph says, but this time his voice is stronger, steadier, more affirmative. Fresh natural air renews his strength. He stands on his own as Stella follows him out.

"I hear the coming of the Bitcoin Era," the Sycophant says. For one last time, he is bent over. Then, "Let the world fill with wealth as I give birth to the new financial order."

The Sycophant lets go an enormous fart that can be heard miles away from the Dollartorium.

"Money, money, money, money …"

The entire Dollartorium begins to shake. More cracks appear in the floor of the mighty Dollartorium, crawl up the walls and cross the arching dome.

The dome, the very foundations, the seats, the scoreboard, the ring, the grand waiting room, the fragile floor, all the machines, and the bolts that hold this place to the earth begin to loosen. The Sycophant doesn't notice, nor would it care if it did. It is swept up into its own trance as the adoring acolytes clap, holler, and cheer, blowing horns, and waving flags. Money is being created at a breathtaking pace. Gobs of money. That's all that matters. Money for themselves. The Sycophant climbs back on its machine and attempts to run it, pretending it controls it, because, as long as it works, no one grows richer than it, and it yearns to be the richest one ever.

Machines inside are going wild. The lights go off. There is fog. Another fart is loosed upon the world, by whom, perhaps by all and all at once. That is something we will never know. Ralph and Stella have crawled to their freedom.

Inside, the chant. "Money." "Money." "Money."

Perhaps someone inside strikes a match to light a cigar.

"No! No!"

The place explodes. Outside Stella and Ralph watch it collapse

"It stinks," Stella says.

It does.

Part 6

THE JOURNEY HOME

Ralph and Stella have escaped the Dollartorium and are headed home. Ralph remains dazzled by all that he learned and has yet to forget. For a moment he had his own money machine. For a moment, he was making millions of dollars, or at least he imagined he was making millions of dollars. At least for a moment, he felt he was rich. But then it all imploded. He does not dare look back. Ralph's clothes are blackened from the explosion that blew out the windows and the doors, through cracks, lifted the roof and fell back on the place. Ralph's body aches from the impact of the explosion which was powerful even standing outside. Stella pulls him along the narrow path back to town. It is morning and they will soon be needed at the Corny Doo Doggery.

"Corn dog," Ralph keeps saying as Stella helps him remember what the world was like before the catastrophe.

"Yes, Daddy. We make corn dogs. We work at the Corny Doo Doggery. We dip the dogs. We cook them. We sell them. And every corn dog we make makes the world a better place. There are few things in this world worse than hunger, after all."

"Yes," Ralph says. He follows along, a few steps behind, lost in thought, trying to remember all that has happened, and before that what it was like making the best corn dogs he's ever tasted.

There's a bounce to his gate as his brain reconnects with his heart.

"With a squiggle of mustard," Ralph says with delight. "Yes. I think I'd like to have a corn dog now."

"Good," Stella says. "We should be home in time for lunch."

"Corn dogs," Ralph says. This time he licks his lips, then he picks up speed to catch up with Stella who walks briskly along, happy to get away from that place and those people who had captured her mother's and father's imaginations.

"Corn dogs. Corn Dogs," Ralph repeats over and over, as if these are new words to him, fresh and warm, as if he had seen freshly dipped. He begins to piece together how it once was, and he rediscovers the warm feelings of how things were before that demon Master came out of the television.

"Yes, Daddy. Corn dogs. I think you may have forgotten what they were like. We made them, you know. You may have the joy of rediscovering what is delicious. Good, fresh pork stuffed in a weenie, dipped in fresh cornmeal batter, and fried. Then we hang them to dry and sell them to our friends. You know they're fresh when you see them dipped."

There is a pause as the fog settles in Ralph's memory and he recalls the good life to which he returns. Slowly they make their way back down the mountainside. It is spring, and everywhere things are green, and it is cool when they pass under the shade of trees. Stella refuses to stop. There will be no resting until they gain distance between themselves and the Dollartorium. Every step takes them closer to home.

"Stella," Ralph says, stopping in the path. "Do we make any money when we sell corn dogs? Do you think I should go back to that place? I was in the middle, I remember, of making a plan …"

Stella frowns to let him know he's regressing, and that she is not going to let him go back. You can save your father once, but she doesn't want it to become a habit. Still, he waits for her answer.

"We've lost everything, haven't we, dear Stella?" Ralph says. "I remember a frenzy and then this huge explosion."

"Nothing burned in that fire is a loss to anyone," Stella says.

"Fire?" Ralphs says. "Oh, yes. Now I remember."

"Maybe a few dollars and a lot of ideas went up in smoke," Stella says. "But the dollars were false, and the ideas were bad. We have a Corny Doo Doggery, Daddy, and a reputation for making them from our special recipe. We are fortunate that, except for this recent wasted time and the price of a ticket, nothing important has changed. Soon we will be back among those good people who are willing to work, and when they work, they do it right and do it for the good of all. Such a way of thinking is invaluable, but all too easily corrupted."

They stop to rest after a few hours of hiking home. They are sitting on a large stone when Ralph sniffs the air.

"What is that I smell?" Ralph asks.

"Probably fresh air," Stella says. "You were in that Dollartorium for too long. Too many people there and too many stinking ideas."

"It's not that, Stella," Ralph says.

He sniffs. Stella stands and sniffs, too. Father and daughter are much alike, in their minds, hearts, and senses, and when one of them is thinking something, most likely the other is thinking that, too.

"Smoke," she says. "Now I see it. Over there."

She points in the distance from where they have come. It is coming from the side of that mountain atop the rock walls where the Dollartorium had once been. Now it was just a column of smoke.

"Do you see it, Daddy?" Stella asks.

He does. "Smoke, indeed," he says. "Dark, and foul. It stinks. Maybe we should report it …"

Ralph turns as if he is going to hurry to town, but Stella holds him back.

"Let it burn," she says. "It's no loss. And anyway, I'm sure those who survive will find a way to put out the fire and rebuild that place. Those types are creative. Greed has its power. But for the rest of us, it will be good to have time free to work without having to put up with their nonsense."

Ralph's face is long and grey. It looks like he has aged a dozen years since he left to find the Dollartorium. But as he relaxes, his youth and vigor seem to be returning. It is his healthy attitude coming back.

"Yes," he says. There is a nostalgia in his voice. "It won't be missed. But I am a little afraid of what your mother is going to say. I went into that world broke, and I've come out of it a bit broker."

Now, hearing those words, Stella is confident her father is on his way to sanity. She gives him a hug.

"Those machines," she says. "And the people who operate

them, flying around in their balloons, cavorting on television, passing gas, the less we have to do with them, the better off we'll be."

She shakes her head but stops talking. She is encouraging him not to remember the details of his experiences. He will need time to heal.

"The world will get along well enough without all that," Stella says. "At least I will. I'll have time to recover my wits and get some real work done."

"They'll be back," Ralph says. "I agree."

He shakes his head and looks down to see his book.

"This," he says, looking at his copy of *Plato, On the Good*. "I'm beginning to wonder if the world of ideas and forms is all that much better than the world that's actually real. Abstractions like money easily delude us."

Stella offers no opinion. Whatever the strength of truth and nature, delusions come easier than reason to some, and delusions can be pleasing to those who are deluded, as if they are comforting ideas to hang onto, if only for a fleeting moment.

"Maybe it's time to change philosophers," she says.

FINAL ACT

Of course, it is hard for us to imagine that Phyllis has been running the Corny Doo Doggery by herself. So, it is quite a surprise when, halfway home, Stella and her father see Phyllis coming up the road to meet them. She wears a tall baker's hat, an apron, and working shoes covered in cornmeal.

"Where have you two been?" she asks. "I've been working at the Doggery all day by myself."

"You worked?" Stella asks. "You opened the store? You made the dogs?"

Stella finds that hard to believe. Ralph has been afraid of the shoe his wife will drop when she finds out he is not yet rich and probably never will be.

"I did," she says. "I might add that yesterday I ran it all by myself."

In fact, Phyllis is not angry. In fact, she seems pleased with herself. In fact, if anything, she seems grateful to discover how much she can do and do well if she tries.

"I didn't think I could do it, but I did. And ..." here she pauses, "I enjoyed it."

She smiles as she joins them on their way home.

"I thought after closing I'd better come rescue you two,"

she says. "Even though it moved, the lunch line at the Doggery doesn't move as fast as it should when you work alone. But people understood. And the corn dogs were as good as ever. I dipped them, cooked them, wrapped them up. I … Well," she continues, "I didn't kill any pigs. I'm not going to kill any pigs. I'll leave that sort of work for you two to do when you all get home. I know my limits. And there wasn't time to do much with the corn. How do you grind that stuff anyway?"

"I'm sorry, Mama, but I had to leave. Father was …"

"You wouldn't believe us, my dear," Ralph says apologetically, "if we told you … Maybe some evening, after an honest day's work, instead of watching television, we will tell each other stories."

Ralph has come back around to normal.

"All by myself," Phyllis says. "You should have seen me, stuffing, dipping, drying. Them customers liked them, too. I never looked at them customers before. Not really. I looked at their money, but not in their faces. And there they were, biting into those corn dogs, you know. Like cats with wet food, they bit into the corn dogs and purred. Yes. I could hear them purr."

It dawns on both Stella and Ralph that, indeed, Phyllis has worked a whole shift by herself and was successful and pleased. Necessity divorced her from her cash register in order to feed the customers so she could charge them for something, but the whole effort soon became more than just taking their money. She had to make something to sell with only herself to rely on. In that she found purpose. And through purpose, satisfaction. And in satisfaction, a grand corn dog. And pleasure in others for all she had done.

"I'm proud of you," Stella says.

They paused for a hug on the trail home. Maybe this was their first hug ever. Certainly Phylllis' first hug in a long time. Phyllis was not to be praised too highly, of course, for doing what obviously needed to be done, but she deserved to be heard as she expressed her discovery of what work could be, and what it could mean.

"I made the whole corn dog, Stella," Phyllis says. "I dipped them—took a while to get the knack of that—cooked them, wrapped them, sold them. And you know what?" she asks.

She pauses as if waiting for an answer, but she doesn't wait long, just enough to let Ralph and Stella grow anxious.

"It's not so bad," Phyllis says. "This work thing."

"It's not?" Stella says, surprised at her mother's discovery. "I'm glad it's not."

"Nope," Phyllis says. "I got those dogs out of the cooler and I stuck them, pushed those little sticks up their ... undersides, I call it."

"You did this alone?" Ralph asks. "No one made you?"

"Well, at first I thought I had to have something to sell if I was going to get paid. Then I thought, look at all them people, waiting for corn dogs. So, I thought, I better get to getting and make some if I can. I've seen you two—in between you reading your books there, Ralph—so I started to think, why not me? Why not try? What's holding me back from doing what needs to be done? Then I thought, if I could do this, I could fire you two and save the labor costs. Then I started doing it, to see what would happen, seeing those people bite into those dogs, some even coming back for a second corn dog … That did it for me. That was reward enough. It got so, from time to time, I almost forgot to charge them.”

“You didn't make them pay?”

“Oh, they paid. I'm not *that* fond of work. Not yet. But the whole cycle, of doing something totally, the whole process you see, there was pleasure in that. So there at the end, the part where they pay, is just them saying to me, 'Thank you, ma'am, for the dog.' Like applause at the end of a good play.”

“You've been reading philosophy,” Stella says.

“Not yet,” Phyllis says. “Let's just say I enjoyed myself. I'd dip and fry and sell. They'd line up, and I'd yell back, 'Corn dogs!' but who was there to get them. So I'd run to the grease pots, dip and fry, then wrap them and deliver, then get to the register to ring them up.”

“My do-all mama.”

“And that's when I discovered, Ralph, we're rich. We're really rich. What a joy it is to see a thing through from beginning to end, to work, and to see a payoff for that work at the end, the thanks one gets so one can do it all again, for myself and for our friends. I'd like to keep on being rich like that forever.”

ENDGAME

Every story comes to some conclusion, or it isn't a story. It's just life, and who cares about that muddle. So, our story could end here, on our hero's journey home, not yet at work, not yet at the Doggery, but close enough they can imagine the crowd gathering again tomorrow at noon as they wait for the Doggery to open. As Stella, Ralph, and Phyllis come closer to town, they feel the anxiety in the crowd, sense their customers' appetite for corn dogs, and for the story to conclude so we can settle down to some good eating. But we all gasp in unison when at last we see our tired and dirty trio, Phyllis in an apron dirty from cornmeal, splattered in grease, Stella and Ralph dressed in rags, singed by flames from the exploding fart, soot on their faces and streaks of sweat down their cheeks.

It has been a struggle, but the three are smiling now as they draw near to home.

"Look," Ralph says, nodding towards the Doggery.

"It's going to be a good day, Daddy," Stella says. "Are we ready?"

The three of them, along with the crowd, can hardly wait for the new normal to morph into an even newer normal. Perhaps, despite all their trials, things will be good.

Maybe because of their trials, things will never have been better.

"Corny Doos will be a-coming," Ralph says to all of us waiting at his store. He wipes his hands on his apron as if cleaning his hands to get ready to work.

The hungry crowd is heartened to see them cross the bridge and enter town. We have no idea of Ralph's troubles. What can we know about other people's lives and their struggles? But we do know a good corn dog when we see it, and we are willing to wait patiently for the family to come home and heat up the fryers.

At last, at the outskirts of town, Ralph looks back to see the distance he has come, and he is the first to see they are being followed. Someone is coming after them, following the same path they have taken. He is pushing a wooden cart, its wheels rumbling over the bridge on the road to the Doggery. Like Ralph and Stella, the man is dressed in dirty singed rags, once a sparkly green, and he is selling corn dogs from his wagon.

"Corn dogs cheap!" the vendor hollers. "Foot longs and regulars! Pretzel buns for ten cents more!"

"Oh, my," Stella says. "We have hardly started up again, and we've got competition."

"Get your Corn Dogs here!" the vendor shouts out. "Imported Corn Dogs! Made 100% with all kinds of stuff! All real, all natural, nothing immaterial in these delicious dogs."

"Nothing unnatural," Stella says with a sneer. "Wood pulp. Coal tar. Benzoate."

"Is that who I think it is?" Phyllis asks. The three of

them have stopped in the road to stare at the competition as he approaches. His cart wobbles its way down the path, the vendor hollering out, "Chewy corn dogs! Freshly thawed! Thirty flavors, sweet and salty!"

"Ah," Phyllis says. "It's him again. The man from the television."

She is no longer infatuated by this media clown who no longer wears a fancy hat and is coated with sparkles that have burnt edges. She is not to be taken in by his fast talk, never again. She is, in fact, angry, for she has wasted her time with his promises and all. She's done with this one.

"My goodness, Daddy," Stella says. "Isn't that the very fella that talked Mama into sending you to that Dollartorium? We paid him a lot and what did we get? What is he doing here? What does he want? And look, he's selling corn dogs! He's after our customers."

"I'm not worried," Ralph says. Back on his home turf and ready to resume his work, Ralph has fully recovered.

"Ralph, Ralph, Ralph!" the Money Master says as he approaches the three of them. He's all smiles and hype. It is the Master, indeed, most of his spangles blown off his clothes, his hat missing its crown, a toe peeking out of his shoe, his hat singed from the flames of the explosion. He has followed them all the way from the Dollartorium, pushing his wooden cart along the dusty road. "Fancy meeting you here. And the lovely Phyllis, as well. And I suppose this is your lovely daughter ..."

He sticks out his hand, but no one takes it.

"You can't have our customers," Stella says.

"It's a free market," he says.

He gives Stella a lascivious look. "I could use you in my marketing campaign. Get you in a bathing suit, put you in some ads … Want a job?"

She doesn't answer.

"I'm starting over," the Money Master continues. He has no shame. "I'm using your marketing plan, Ralph, and a great plan it is. I'll start right here, smack dab in the middle of Main Street, just this side of the corn field, first with a humble cart, selling fancy imported corn dogs shipped straight from Vietnam, made mostly with pork and cornbread, some artificial sweeteners, flavored with any of a dozen syrup flavors, with preservatives that will keep them fresh for a hundred years guaranteed, stuck with plastic sticks instead of wood, no splinters, some chicken filler in there, and I don't know what else. It's hard to remember what all we ground up. But it's good. And good for you. Frozen and shipped to America! America! Indeed, to be eaten in America! By Americans! I call them American Dogs. Or Freedom Dogs. Who in America doesn't want a Freedom Dog? I've borrowed money from the bank, and tomorrow I'll have a store, and …"

"You're selling corn dogs," Ralph says. He's disgusted. "You're a thief. You've stolen my plan and now you plan to steal my business."

"Your business, Ralph?" he says incredulously. "Now, how could I have known that, like yours is the only corn dog that ever was or ever will be? And let's not start flinging words around like a thief, or something. I got lawyers, Ralph. I've never lost a case. I'll sue you, Ralph. Let's say, I've simply modified what's possibly a great American success story. I may write a book: The Art of the Corn

Dog."

"I thought the Dollartorium was making you rich," Phyllis says.

"Oh, that old thing," the Master says. "Well, it's gone. Gone, gone, gone. Blew up, burned down, collapsed, I'm told, it all happened in a fit of greed and jealousy. One of my students tried making too much too quickly, with too little time, with too many bills, with too much debt, and prices rose, and prices fell, and I never noticed until too late that an idiot was at the wheel of the economy. I tell you it is dangerous when people want more when there is no more and borrow too much when there is not enough to lend. Well—the machine caught fire and the whole place has been reduced to ashes. I need to start over, and I'm back to ideas and forms."

Stella chortles. "That's Plato. Well, fortunately for us we're changing philosophers."

"Don't worry, dear," the Master says. "Buy a corn dog. You won't regret it. Selling hot dogs. It's the best idea I've ever stolen."

"I'd think you'd have the courtesy to come up with your own ideas," she says.

"I'd like to get you on a poster," he says. "'Women love Freedom Dogs. And the men who ...' A tight little swimsuit. Bend over just a little. I'd like to see ..."

"I'm busy," she says. "The pigs need feeding. And we need to open up the doors for our customers."

Indeed, their customers have gathered around and are now applauding. "Feed the pigs! Feed the pigs!" The crowd is hungry and eager for this discussion to end, as well as this story, so they can dig into lunch.

"Oh, go ahead, go ahead," the Master says. He pushes his cart along, singing out, "Freedom Dogs! Freedom Dogs! Genuine imported, only once frozen, mostly natural, nothing immaterial, Freedom Dogs!"

He can be heard rolling his cart down the street as he mutters to himself.

"First thing I'm gonna do is smash the competition across the river," he continues as his cart rumbles back across the bridge. He turns around to Ralph. "And that's you, buddy boy, and that cutie you got working for you," the Master says. "Then I'm going to open a fancy stand in the suburbs, expand the product line, add a chili corn dog with cheese. Start a food stand near the hospital—corn dogs, chili dogs, franks, and wieners. 'All my pigs are organic.' Now, there's a line a mother can love. One stand near the University. 'Fat and sassy Jumbo Dogs.' I like that." He stops to write that down. "All organic, because what's more organic than a pig."

He resumes his hawking and his walking.

"I'll get ads at the Super Bowl ..."

He wanders onto the dirt road across the bridge, almost to the edge of town.

"During the sweet sixteen, I'll have women in tight little outfits, so when they bend forward, you tell yourself, 'if she bends just a little bit more, I'll be able to see her ...'"

But then he is too far away to be heard at all and barely visible.

"I'll feed the pigs, Daddy. You better turn the grease pots on."

Then the cart turns a corner and is out of sight.

"He's out to smash us," Phyllis says.

"Don't worry," Ralph says. "We make a better corn dog. And we'll teach people that that means something. Meanwhile …"

"… the corn needs picking," Stella says. "And that's good, honest work."

"I think I'm done with Plato for a while. I think I'll give Wittgenstein a read. Things are pretty chaotic, but at least back home things are things, and not ideas."

"Put on your hat, Daddy," Stella says as soon as they enter the Doggery. They have unlocked the door, laid out the dogs, and fired up the grease. They are going to have a busy lunch.

Phyllis resets the register, then reaches up—but stops. She does not turn on the television. "That thing's been nothing but trouble," she says. "Today I'm just going to try talking to our customers again."

Soon the doors are open, and, for the next few hours, you find yourself among the many customers who line up for service. There are more of us today than usual. Perhaps Ralph's little absence from the store has stirred our appetites. Many of us promise to come back tomorrow. The corn dogs are as good as ever. They could have sold them all, but today they held back a few. On her way to the bank, Phyllis stopped by one of the places she knows and shared the last remaining dogs with those in need, a gift to those who have less for now, and for some who might never have relished the best.

ABOUT RON PULLINS

RON PULLINS is a writer working in Tucson AZ. His works have been published in numerous journals including Typishly (Editor's Choice), Southwest Review, Shenandoah, Sunspot, etc., and been nominated for Pushcart. Pullins won the 2022 Malcolm Lowry award for *Dollartorium*, Unsolicited Press, 2026. His novellas, *Ice Dancing* and *Fracture* have been published in *SunSpot Literary* magazine. A novel in progress, *The Loin*, was featured in a radio podcast by Mauhaus Productions, 2025.

ABOUT THE PRESS

Unsolicited Press is based out of Portland, Oregon and focuses on the works of the unsung and underrepresented. As a womxn-owned, all-volunteer small publisher that doesn't worry about profits as much as championing exceptional literature, we have the privilege of partnering with authors skirting the fringes of the lit world. We've worked with emerging and award-winning authors such as Amy Shimshon-Santo, Brook Bhagat, Elisa Carlsen, Tara Stillions Whitehead, and Anne Leigh Parrish.

Learn more at unsolicitedpress.com. Find us on Instagram, X, Facebook, Pinterest, Bsky, Threads, YouTube, and LinkedIn. Unsolicited Press also writes a snarky newsletter on Substack.

www.ingramcontent.com/pod-product-compliance
Lightning Source LLC
Chambersburg PA
CBHW061247310726
48971CB00007B/2254